THE MERMAID UPSTAIRS

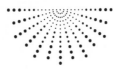

JAMI LILO

PROLOGUE

"I know, Nora. I signed the contract," I answered my mother as I turned on my blinker instead of the windshield wipers. Darn it! Why didn't I read the instruction manual like she said too? Why was she always right?

"Emily, if you don't know the rules, how can you follow them? A contract..." my mother started, pulling her stray hairs into her tight bun as she spoke.

"...confirms everyone is on the same page. I know, Nora, you've been drafting contracts since I was seven. I was the only kid in elementary school signing contracts with my crayons." Why did my mother have to be an attorney? Life would be so much easier if she was something else. Anything else. Why couldn't my mother be a hair stylist? I hate her stupid bun.

She leaned over from the passenger seat and twisted the knob on the steering wheel, turning on the windshield wipers. "Did you know these were invented by a woman? Mary Anderson, I believe. She called them window cleaning devices."

I watched the few droplets of rain pelting down from the Nebraska sky be swiped away. Nora was a living encyclopedia on top of being a ball-busting attorney.

"You can't expect the men in your life to carry their weight, Em." She sighed and I exhaled loudly, hoping my disapproval of her venting about my dad yet again was shown through my gust of huffy air.

"I'll need you to pick up Amy from dance at three," she said, sorting through files and using my passenger seat as her makeshift office.

"I just got my driver's license, Nora. I want to go to the mall. Maybe a coffee shop. Things normal teenagers do. Not just pick up my little sister."

"Normal teenagers refer to their mothers as mom and your definition of normal is actually privileged," Nora said before sticking a file into her mouth, thankfully ending her lecture.

"I'm not spoiled if I have an ice-blended. It's coffee. I'm allowed to have a coffee without you making me feel bad about all the kids in the world who have nothing." My hands gripped the steering wheel as the rain pelted down harder.

Since she didn't respond I knew I'd lost her to her phone. Work always sucked her away.

"I'll pick up Amy." I started, "...and then go to the mall. Deal, Nora?"

Nora took a deep breath and removed the file from her mouth, leaving an imprint of her signature burnt-brick lipstick where her lips had been. She moved her mouth, but no words came out. The skin on her neck looked splotchy, like a rash was creeping up to her cheeks.

"Mom?" I looked at the road and pumped the breaks before stopping at a red light. "What's wrong?"

"I.." was all Nora said. She opened the file that had been in her mouth, looked over something inside and then closed it, swallowing so hard I could hear it. The lip stain on the folder was the last thing I saw as we were struck by a car from behind.

BAM.

A driver was looking down, "AKA texting" and rammed into my rear bumper leaving a dent the size of a golf ball. I was fine, at least I felt completely normal. But my mother hit her head on the window and she was still clutching the lipstick stained file when they loaded her into ambulance.

"She's going to be okay, Em," My dad assured me as we watched the ambulance speed away. Fortunately, he hadn't left for his conference yet and actually beat the police to what they were referring to as the accident site.

But the funny feeling in my stomach said that she wasn't okay. In fact, by the flip-flops my intestines were doing, I somehow knew, my mother, Nora, would never be the same again.

CHAPTER ONE

"You were in a car accident right after you got your license?" Kessia hissed, making a face that could be a meme.

I nodded and then pointed to where Mr. Edwards was standing. I was already discombobulated from being late for school and my disasterous morning. The last thing I wanted was to get detention for talking in class too.

Kessia's jaw dropped dramatically before she scribbled something with furious speed onto a piece of paper and passed it to me.

OMG Emily! Is your mom okay?

She scanned my face for freak-out level, but I was still in information processing mode.

My dad said she's acting fishy.

I don't think anyone could have known what he meant by that. Did she smell rank? Was she acting peculiar? Eating worms? My mother, Nora, the attorney at Child Protective Services did not act fishy, so I had nothing to associate that description with. What I gathered was she still had control of all her limbs and bodily functions, and so I went to school like any normal day.

Little did I know, my mother had gone off the deep end.

Kessia's note back to me was taking on book form, so I tried to focus on Mr. Edward's Shakespeare lesson, but my brain refused to cooperate and my fingers hurt from keeping them in tight fists since my accident. Maybe I wasn't as okay as I thought.

Mr. Edwards swiped the note out of Kessia's hand mid-pass, "Ten-point deduction, Emily and Kessia." Without missing a beat, he continued, "Class project partners will be announced tomorrow. Read the remaining assigned pages; do not attempt to Google or SparkNotes your way out of this. Read Shakespeare's actual words."

"Sorry, Em," Kessia mouthed as we filed out of class.

"It's okay," I said, but she knew I'd beat myself up about it. I hated getting in trouble. Maybe because my mother is an attorney, I've always been a goodie-good. One of those kids that always did what I was supposed to do. I like rules. I even read the instruction booklets everyone else tosses.

Dad texted an update while I picked out the salvageable turkey from my drenched brown bagged sandwich. *Pick your sister up from school and make dinner. I don't know what time your mother will be released from the hospital. Please and thank you.*

My mom was in the hospital, acting fishy...still. Closing my eyes, I tried to remember the last thing I'd said to her this morning.

"You okay, Sleeping Beauty?" Kessia asked, placing a hot tray of prison worthy food onto the table in front of her.

"My stomach acid could boil hotdogs."

"Why don't you skip sixth period and go check on her? You're worthless here." She stuffed overcooked tater tots into her mouth.

"I can't, we have a quiz." I never ditched class, it gave me too much anxiety to be truant.

"Emily! Your mother is in the hospital!"

"My dad swears she's fine." I lied a bit, but it could be true. Mom could be home before dinner for all I knew.

But she wasn't home before dinner, or even after I loaded our dirty plates into the dishwasher.

Like any evening when mom had to work late, I tucked my little sister, Amy, into bed. It didn't happen often, but when it did I'd pretend I was mature and responsible beyond my sixteen years of age. I fantasized that my handsome husband, José, was in the dining room waiting for me with a glass of wine and a cheeseburger. It was always José in my make-believe future. I'd been infatuated with him for as long as I could remember. Only tonight was different because my mother wasn't working and I didn't know what was happening.

"Where is mom, Emily?" Amy asked for the millionth time. The decade sized age gap between us felt like light-years.

"Dad said they'd be home in an hour, and it's already past your bedtime. Let's go," I nodded toward her bedroom, using my best mom voice.

"I want mom," she repeated.

After singing Selena Gomez songs until she passed out, I went to my room to finish my homework. Since reading Shakespeare is the cure for insomnia, I too slipped into a semi-deep slumber until I heard crying.

And splashing.

Creeping down the hallway to the master bedroom, I tip-toed into my parent's sanctuary. The light was on in the master bathroom and so I inched closer. *Was that my mother crying? Why did she keep saying the salt wasn't working?*

I pushed the door ajar just a tad, giving a light courtesy knock and spooking my father. He was holding my mother's hand and shushing her like a baby. "It'll be okay. We'll figure this out."

"Dad, what's going on?"

My mother tossed a rubber duck from the tub and it landed

amongst many empty bags of Epson salt scattered around the tile floor.

He looked up at me, his knees wet and one shoe off, before simply stating as if it were completely normal, "Your mother thinks she is a mermaid."

"You did it again!" my mother shrieked like a wounded bird, kicking her legs, sending waves of water onto the tile.

Nora never shrieked. Nora never lost her cool. Who was this woman who had taken over my mother's body? Why did she sound like a Pterodactyl?

"My beautiful tail," she blubbered, pointing to her legs. "It's aqua and turquoise with flecks of gold in the sunlight. Oh my magnificent tail…" her voice trailed off.

"I stand corrected; I'm so sorry," my father said, defeated. With pleading eyes, begging me to understand and go along with the craziness unfolding before me, he continued, "Emily, your mother IS a mermaid."

CHAPTER TWO

My mother tried to convince me that she usually has a turquoise-blue tail with gold flecks that sparkle in the sunlight.

"I need my tail," she squawked, her voice cracking with despair as she stared at her bare feet. Her dark hair stuck to the sides of her face and her clothes clung to her body as she sat shivering in an overflowing bathtub. "Take me back to the ocean...or I'll die!"

"I don't think mermaids exist, Mom." I treaded lightly, not wanting to upset her further, as I collected a pile of wet towels from the floor, "...at least not in the suburbs of Nebraska."

Stifling nervous laughter, I turned to dad. "What is she on?"

"Emily, your mother..." He ran his hands through his wet hair, exhaling. "You know what, kiddo? I'll clean up. You need to get some rest."

"Like I could sleep after seeing...this." My pajamas absorbed the moisture from the wet towels I held, but I couldn't take my eyes off my mother. I don't think I've seen her without her hair slicked back in a bun in ages. And I've never seen her splash around like a giraffe stuck in a tank; long limbs flailing about. It was jolting. "Is she going to be okay?"

"Good as new. You'll see." Dad forced a smile and patted my back for reassurance. "Off to bed, young lady."

For the rest of the night, my normally cozy bed felt lumpy and uncomfortable as if sleeping in a ball pit. After tossing and turning for hours, I crawled to the pantry and shoveled Special K into my mouth while I sleep-watched an exercise infomercial on the couch, both wishing sleep would take me and yet hoping I would wake from this nightmare.

IN THE MORNING, Dad shuffled in as I brushed Amy's hair into a ponytail. With two cups of coffee and a gallon of vanilla creamer to sustain me, I was wired enough to get both myself and sister ready for school. Dad, on the other hand, looked like he'd been beaten in a cage fight, deep blue circles shone under each eye.

"I'm taking a few days off from work, Em. It's going to be a lot of doctor appointments, tests, and what not." He threw back his coffee and gulped it down."Okay," I said, finishing Amy's hair. "Hope those drugs she was on last night have worn off."

"Keep it between us, Em, K?" He didn't have to tell me to keep my mother's warped delusion that she has a mermaid tail to myself. Did he really think I'd post something like that on social media? It's not like I'm popular, but I'd like to keep flying below radar. Invisible is still slightly better than total loser.

"Got it," I shot him with my finger and gave an exaggerated wink before bringing him a new cup of coffee.

He nodded. "Thanks, Em."

"Where's mom?" Amy whined, racing over to my dad and hugging him.

"Asleep," he hugged her back as if it had been years and not hours since he'd seen her. "She'll be all better this afternoon when you get home from school."

But when I caught his eye, I saw something that caught me completely off guard. Fear.

AFTER DROPPING off Amy at the elementary school, Kessia and I stopped in Dunkin' Donuts. Against my better judgment, I had a third cup of coffee with hazelnut while Kessia stuffed a half dozen donut holes in her mouth. She then posted a post-donut selfie she tagged #DonutsAreLife.

Kessia probably has posted close to 2,000 selfies. A close up of her tonsils, half-chewed food in her mouth, a side boob...you name it. Pretty much whatever she feels like in the moment, and then she's off to the next thing.

I have exactly two pictures on my social media account, both of which I obsessed over until my eyes bled. Then, the waiting for pity "likes" to happen was traumatizing enough to turn me into a lurker and not an active participant in social media. My motto, "no posting, no roasting," keeps me safely off the high school grid.

By the time English came around, I was jittery and tweaking, sucking Altoids to calm my acidic stomach. Mr. Edwards showed no mercy, announcing project partners first thing.

"You'll find your partner's name at the top of the sheet, and the project specifications below."

I scoured the sheet for my name to find: Emily Parker, José Hernandez

My name was with José's name. Not exactly how I pictured it on our wedding invitations, but close enough. I was partnered with José. I popped two more Altoids into my mouth so my stomach wouldn't explode and tried not to hyperventilate.

It was fate. We were so 'Romeo' and 'Juliet.' Well, if only he didn't have a girlfriend.

Kessia made a face at me that only I could understand. Translation: *You're partnered with your soul mate!* She internally cheered for me like the best friend she is.

"What are you picking for a topic choice, Miss Kessia?" asked Mr. Edwards, breaking our telekinesis spell.

Kessia searched the room for Jack, her assigned partner, then spoke, "I'd need to consult with my better half."

"Jack?" Mr. Edwards interjected.

Stud Muffin Jack played along, grinning at Kessia. "Happy wife, happy life." He reveled in the enthusiastic level of laughter he'd earned.

"Okay," Mr. Edwards nodded, "Reminder, it's a partnership. I want to see Jack's fifty percent contribution." He wiped his nose on his homemade handkerchief and tucked it into his pant pocket. Mr. Edwards seemed to have an endless stream of snot draining from his nose. He'd proclaim ever so often that he has chronic allergies, but I wondered if he just caught every single cold we passed around at school. Sometimes I worried I'd get sick after he graded my papers and got his germs all over them, but so far I've remained healthy.

He circled the classroom, choosing his next victim, thankfully not me. It's a good thing since I could hardly form a sentence. My near caffeine overdose and the thought of working with José was sending an adrenaline cocktail through my veins. My thoughts jumped around my head, my insecurities blasting like Coachella taking place in my brain. What if José thinks I'm stupid? I'm not one of those brainiacs who has an extensive vocabulary. I am devoted to spell check. Reliant really. And, I have no idea what Shakespeare is saying. Ever. I was finally going to get to spend an extensive amount of time with my crush, but he'd quickly learn I am inept when it comes to the Elizabethan Age. It's almost like I don't even understand English. Why had Mr. Edward's partnered us? It was so awesome, and yet so disastrously awful.

I couldn't wait to get advice from mom; she'd be able to

calm my nerves. Hopefully she was feeling better and we could put this entire mermaid episode behind us. Although I couldn't erase the image of my mother in the overflowing bathtub, I planned to pretend it never happened. Sure, my mother swearing she had a tail and would die if she didn't return to the Pacific Ocean would probably live in some deep crevice of my mind forever, but if I could delete the memory entirely, I would.

CHAPTER THREE

"What is that smell?" Mom covered her mouth as she walked into the kitchen with my father. Dad had taken her to a number of doctors and had tests run. I quickly assessed that she looked absolutely fine, not even a bandage on her head or a limp.

"Mommy!" Amy cried and tackled her like a mini-linebacker.

"Fried shrimp. Ready in five minutes," I waved my hand that was encased with a lobster claw oven mitt. "Feeling better?"

Mom stood awkwardly while Amy hugged her. She patted Amy's head like a dog with one hand, covering her mouth with the other.

"The smell," she squeaked from behind her hand.

"Um. Sorta," Dad interjected. "It's gonna take some time."

"What does that mean? She looks fine," I observed, my voice rising to dolphin octaves. "Wait, do you have internal bleeding? Are you dying?"

"Mommy's dying!" Amy screamed.

"No. Stop it, Emily. No one is dying," he sat at the table. "Amy, come sit with me, Sweetheart."

Amy let go of mom and flew into the comfort of Dad's arms. She'd always been the baby in the family, but this crisis was sending her back to fetus status. I could see therapy in her future. Years perhaps.

"I can't eat that," Mom cringed, backing toward the door. "I love all sea creatures."

Though I'm not always the best at reading situations, even I could tell this was not the time to remind Nora that the muffin top she was sporting over her leggings came from years of binging at the Friday Night Seafood buffet. Shrimp tempura and crab cakes to be exact, but apparently she didn't remember stuffing her face with her beloved sea creatures last weekend.

"Nora, please sit down. Emily will make you a nice salad," Dad coaxed. "Emily, grab a salad pack and throw it in a bowl, please." His tone screamed, *Don't mess with me, I'm dog-tired.*

Nora smiled weakly and joined us at the table. Not wanting to lose my car keys, I jumped up to retrieve the salad. Mom was still acting weird. Distant. She hadn't even said hi to me. And she looked weird. Her hair wasn't styled; it was just dropping around her face, which looked pale, pudgy, and tired. The more I studied her, the more I saw that mom looked exhausted. Yes, she always appeared slightly drained, but now it was full on zombie apocalypse lethargy.

"Thank you," she said when I placed the salad in front of her, as if I were a waitress and not her daughter.

"Sure, Nora. No biggie," I smiled. Then, I burst out my good news, "José Hernandez is my English project partner. Can you believe it?"

Mom has known about my affection for José for ages. I envisioned her happy dance and the joy I'd given her by announcing her future son-in-law.

"Um. That's a good thing?" She wondered out loud.

I nodded. "Duh."

Nora looked at my dad and was silent. My mom was never silent and it was making me uncomfortable. Usually dad would struggle to get a word in edge wise, but tonight Nora was giving him the floor. She seemed to be waiting for him to speak for her. Nora never let anyone speak for her before.

"Emily, your mother's doctors don't know what is going on yet, but they agree things are not clear. Like there's a traffic jam in her brain, keeping the thoughts from flowing freely. Things are a bit fuzzy for her right now."

"How fuzzy, Mommy?" Amy asked, clearly confused. "Can you see me? Does mom need glasses?"

"Not exactly fuzzy. Um...well, she's a mermaid." Dad spat out. My mother smiled warmly at him and placed her hand on his.

"Mommy is a mermaid?!?!" Amy squealed at an octave reserved for six-year-olds.

"How long is it gonna last?" I questioned, realizing I was still wearing the lobster claw oven mitt. Every time I moved my hand around, Mom flinched.

Dad shrugged. His shirt was digging into his armpits and I noticed the sweat stains had rings like trees; they had aged over the years. Why was I being so hypersensitive to my surroundings? Everything seemed smaller and tighter, like we were being squished into the room. Like there was limited air and we had to take turns breathing.

"Shouldn't she be in the hospital...or something?"

"The beds at the hospital are full, with a heavy wait list. It's not like a hotel where we can just check in. And she's not self-harming or a threat to anyone. And honestly, Em, I really think she'll feel better at home with us."

She didn't seem to feel better here.

"Who is going to watch her? You're always working..." So many questions bubbled up inside me at once. Was I going to have to drop out of high school to take care of my mother?

"Em, I don't have any answers right now. I'm kind of winging it," he admitted.

We were all staring at Nora, who just smiled back as us meekly.

"Do you know who we are at all?" I dared ask, not sure if I wanted to hear her answer.

"Not completely," she admitted. "I feel a connection...I'm just not sure what it is."

"But you know who he is?!?" I pointed at Dad.

"Of course I do. He's Bart."

Okay, I relaxed a bit. She remembered dad. She couldn't be too far gone. But then she continued in a dreamy, far away voice, "Bart the Pirate. He saved me...again."

Amy looked back and forth between my parents, "Again, Mommy?"

"The first time, I was just a teen swimming in the Pacific Ocean. I was captured by a gang of dangerous sea thieves and tied to their mast. They wanted me to sing so I would lure a rival ship towards the rocks. But I refused, accepting my fate which would most likely be death."

"Okay, well, you're here. You're fine. She's okay, see, Amy." My dad stumbled over his words, patting Amy reassuringly on the back.

"They were part octopus, the whole gang of them. Black ink dripping out of their eyes..." She held her hands spread open in front of her face and slowly moved them down to dramatically accentuated the ink dripping out of the eyes.

"Nora, please." Dad stopped her from going on about the octopi gang. "She's okay, Amy."

"Unbelievable," I caught myself saying out loud.

"It was," Nora continued. "Bart the Pirate rescued me and I became his forever and ever for eternity."

For the first time in my life that I could recall, I was absolutely speechless.

CHAPTER FOUR

M om's coworker, Janet, took Nora out for the afternoon, so Kessia and I had the place to ourselves. Janet and Nora had worked together at Child Protective Services for almost twenty years and Janet was almost like the Aunt I never had, or wanted. The good news was if anyone could snap Nora out of her mermaid delusion, it was no-nonsense, fun-extinguisher Janet.

"Kessia, where can I take a crash course in all things Shakespeare?"

"How would I know? I have no idea how Jack and I are going to do our project either," Kessia confessed.

"Are you interested in Stud Muffin Jack?" I asked, using our nickname we had given him in middle school.

"Nope." She flipped through my mom's 80s DVD collection like she'd get infected if she touched one of the old movies for too long. "These movies are ancient."

"He's really hot," I nudged her with my elbow and raised my eyebrows up and down. "I'm talking about Stud Muffin Jack."

"Yep. Don't care."

"Kessia, you can't stay single forever because of your Dad."

"All men are pigs. Fact," Kessia crossed her arms over her chest, ready for a confrontation.

"Maybe your Dad just fell in love with someone else. It happens. It sucks, but it happens." I wanted to be gentle with Kessia, but honest. We made a pact in kindergarten that we'd always tell each other the truth, even if it hurts. We agreed it was way worse to keep a secret from each other and later learn the truth on the playground. The truth had a funny way of finding you at recess.

"With a child!?! She's twenty-years-old. Only four years older than his daughter." Kessia grunted. She'd argue with me when I told her my opinions, but she knew I only had her best interest at heart. I was always in her corner.

"Stop regurgitating what your mom said," she griped, and then mimicked me, holding her nose and using what was apparently my mother's voice, "People fall in love with someone else all the time, Kessia." She removed her hand from pinching her nose. "Seriously, stop it, or I'll regurgitate all over you. You know what my dad did to my mom is horrible. And to me!"

"You're right," I exhaled loudly and groaned. "God, how much of my mom's thoughts do I spurt out? Thank you for stopping the madness."

It frightened me to think that my mind went on autopilot with Nora as the driver. My mother was a strong-willed woman with supernatural powers of persuasion. She never lost court cases. And she'd carefully planted her opinion seeds into my head since my conception. So many seeds that I'd be weeding forever to find my own thoughts deep within my cranium.

Kessia knew my mom and I were in the car accident, but she didn't know the full extent of Nora's mental state. Turns out I didn't have to update her because Janet brought my mom in as if she was Makeover Barbie: Mermaid Edition.

Nora's hair had extensions down to her waist, pink ones and blue ones mixed in with her naturally brunette mane. It looked like something you'd find on a child's My Pretty Pony horse tail. Sure, these days tons of people have colorful hair, whether it's extensions or dyed, but this was my mother, who had worn a boring bun for my entire existence. So I could get beyond the passing of the bun, and even the initial shock of her freshly applied spray tan *and* the multi-layered tank top almost hid her muffin top. But the pants, or leggings really, were covered in sequins. Where do you find sequined leggings in Nebraska?

"Wow Nora, you're savage!" Kessia said, punctuating her sentiment with a fox whistle.

Nora spun around for us, swooshing her colorful extensions around her freshly painted face. Amy was delighted and ran to feel her textured legs.

"We decided to go for it!" Janet declared.

Thank you, Janet. My mother now looks as crazy as she sounds.

Janet, the serious, ball-busting feminist had apparently decided to throw out all her beliefs to decorate my mom like a professional mermaid working a child's aquatic themed birthday party.

"I want to look like a mermaid!" Amy begged.

"I picked up a few things for you, Sunshine! Nail polish!" Nora held up bottles full of colorful glitter paint.

Amy squealed and they disappeared down the hall.

Kessia looked at me with her eyes big and mouthed, "Sunshine!?"

How do you explain that your mother whole heartedly believes she belongs in the ocean? I saw Kessia's wheels turning, her brain's think-o-meter about to burst.

"Your mom has extensions! I'm sooooo jelly."

"Kessia, she's not okay." I paused to let this info soak in. "She thinks she's a mermaid from the Pacific Ocean."

"But you guys are like allergic to the sun!"

Kessia and I were always being chased with sunscreen as children. Every summer our mothers purchased a case of SPF 50 and slathered it over our bodies like glue. Public pools could smell us coming from the parking lot. I hated how it stung my eyes as I hit the highly chlorinated water. As we got older, Kessia and I opted for night swimming to avoid being covered in the thick paste.

"A mermaid?" Kessia asked, "Like for real, though?"

"Emily," Janet interrupted us. "I've given your mother some basic skills, but she's going to need a lot of guidance through this time. Call me if she needs *anything.*" Janet placed great emphases on the anything. Yes, we get it Janet, you'd take a bullet for my mother. She grabbed her purse, flung it over her shoulder and headed towards the door. "I mean it, Emily. She's going to need a lot of help."

"Got it," I yelled as she shut the door behind her. It was always a great relief when Janet left, like we could remove the gas masks since the toxic fumes were gone.

Once alone again, Kessia jumped up and down as if celebrating some great victory. "This is soooooooo cool."

"No, it's awful." How could Kessia not see the train wreck this was? It was graphically disturbing and I couldn't get the image of my mother in sequins leggings from behind my eyes.

"Now is your chance to wear cut-offs and your mom won't say a thing. You can eat what you want. Do what you want. Anything!"

"Kessia, this is serious. She's sick."

"She'll be fine. You've probably got a week tops. Live it up before your mom gets her memory back." She slumped onto the couch and threw a pillow at me, annoyed that I wasn't seeing the possibilities of debauchery in my mother's sudden illness.

I hadn't thought of it like Kessia. Maybe it wasn't such a big deal and I should just embrace it. My mom couldn't think she was a mermaid forever. Eventually her memory had to come back and life would return to normal.

"Let me know if some Shakespeare inspiration strikes." She said as she headed to the door and opened it. "You know, Em, you're lucky. I wish my mom would take a mental vacation."

CHAPTER FIVE

O n Sunday I decided I would talk some sense into mom. Maybe spending some time alone with her would trigger her giving birth to me or something. This charade really needed to be over A.S.A.P.

While Dad snored, I invited mom to IHOP. She tried to wake Bart the Pirate for pancakes, but Dad could sleep through anything. Amy wanted to join us and I figured she's young and cute so she'd pull on mom's heart and wake her up faster. We loaded into my car and headed down the road.

"It's so pretty." Mom referred to the paint on my car. "The way the blue and silver flecks sparkle in the sun…like my tail."

"Okay. Yeah I guess," I replied. It was a plain, ol' blue car.

"Is this your car?" She asked, playing with the window knob.

"My parents, one being you, took over payments from our neighbor when his wife passed," I watched her and then the road. She rolled the window all the way down and back up again.

"Oh, I'm so sorry for your loss," she sighed and looked at me again.

"She was nice, but she lived a long life. Babs. You used to

take her meals when she got too sick to cook. You don't remember her? Or her husband, Fred? They have been our next door neighbors my entire life. Fred still lives there."

Nora shook her head. "No, I remember the merpeople, my friends and family in the sea. I miss them."

Great, she missed merpeople.

"My parents, again *you*, would have never gotten me this new of a car, but since you are a stickler for helping others, when Fred asked for your help with the car, I scored. Plus, you wanted me to start driving Amy to and from school. So that worked in my favor."

Nora just listened. At least I think she was listening. She stared at me.

"Don't mermaids blink?"

"Of course we do. I just want to remember my time here." She acted like a tourist visiting her own life.

"Mommy, can I have Funfetti pancakes?" Amy asked from the back seat.

"That's you," I informed Nora of who she was. "You're Mommy."

"Yes," she replied and shrugged, a huge goofy smile on her face.

"You don't even know what they are," I remarked.

"But she wants them. I want her to be happy."

So, that was how Nora was going to parent now. Based on happiness and unicorns and peace signs. Nora, who had always been about doing the right thing. Do your best. Be a good citizen. Maybe I didn't want to wake her up. Maybe this was the best thing to ever happen to us.

Nora ordered Funfetti pancakes for us all and we scarfed them down with four different flavors of syrup. She listened to me talk about José, and Amy talked about her science project, and it was nice. And relaxed. Nora never used to relax. She was too busy saving the world.

"I want a birthday party." Amy went for it.

My plan had been to jolt my mom awake, but Amy was going to be the one to do it. I spent my sixteenth birthday at a homeless shelter making sandwiches. Yes, I got our deceased neighbor's car and I'm extremely grateful, but there was no way Nora was going to suddenly start throwing princess parties and participating in indulgences when she knows how many children go without a single birthday present. Believe me, I know.

It's not that my childhood was depressing or anything like that, but Nora made sure that Amy and I weren't spoiled, materialistic, and that our expectations were exceedingly low. "You wake to privilege every, single day," she had said so many times my brain's storage file had maxed out.

"Sounds like a great idea!" Nora exclaimed, obviously high off the rainbow specks in the Funfetti pancakes.

"What? What?!?! You hate..." Amy kicked me hard and gave me the look of death.

"I want balloons. And a pink cake. And lots of presents. And for you to wear a princess dress."

I decided to give this to Amy. I never had a big princess party, but honestly, I didn't need one. And I could use this to my advantage somehow. It was always good to have your little sister in your pocket.

When the check arrived, Nora pulled out her credit card from her wallet and handed it to the waiter. In the past, Nora would inspect the bill and check the tax to make sure she wasn't being overcharged. When the card returned Nora beamed at us, "It's magical."

"What is? The credit card?" I looked at the booth behind us. Was anyone else hearing this nonsense?

"I just hand it to them and they give me whatever I want. Janet taught me how to use it." She sat up straighter, clearly proud of her accomplishment.

"They send you a bill at the end of the month. You have to pay for it."

She continued to smile. Oblivious.

"With money. You do remember money, right?" I pushed further, leaning closer to her.

"We don't use that. We exchange shells and trinkets," She bent forward and stole another bite of Funfetti from Amy's plate.

"What kind of trinkets?" Amy asked before shoving another scoop of pancakes in her mouth.

"Jewelry. Decorations. Baubles. Gewgaw." Nora traced her fork over her plate, squishing the last bit of pancakes into a smiley face drowning in syrup.

Apparently math isn't used much under water. Shells and trinkets are their currency. And gewgaw. I wondered if this entire underwater fairytale land existed already in her messed up head or if she was making it up as she went along. Nothing about this was making sense. Mom didn't look sick. There wasn't a bump on her head. It was more like she was taken over by an alien or something. Only that alien was a mermaid.

I spoke to Nora as if she were a fragile, baby bird, "You realize we live in Nebraska, right? We are nowhere near the ocean." I pressed harder, showing her a map of Columbus, Nebraska on my iPhone, "See, we are here. Completely landlocked."

Amy waited, her breath held for my mom to suddenly snap back to her old self. But it didn't happen. Instead Nora started rocking uncomfortably and whispered in barely audible sentences.

"How did I get so far from home?"

"We're in Columbus, Nebraska. We're closer to Iowa than any Ocean." I willed her to understand. To snap out of this trance, but she just rocked.

"But I live in the Pacific Ocean," she grew more distraught. "How did I get so far from home?"

Amy rubbed mom's hand, "It's okay, Mom. You're going to be okay. Dad said."

Nora stopped rocking a bit and looked at Amy as if she held

all the answers in the universe. "Will you teach me mermaid language?" Amy cooed.

"I'd love to."

Amy and Nora held hands on the way back to the car.

So what if being a mermaid in the middle of Nebraska was completely absurd. She was still my mom, even if she didn't remember, and as I watched her laugh and smile with Amy, my heart bubbled with so much love for her. And my heart ached. She was right in front of me, but I missed my real mom.

The entire way home, Nora swore she could hear the waves calling to her. But no one has that good of hearing. Not even a mermaid.

CHAPTER SIX

Bart the Pirate informed me of my chauffeuring/babysitting schedule as I ate pigs in a blanket, the only thing I could find in the freezer. My English project schedule with José was already stressing me out, but now Dad was dumping a new pile of responsibility on me.

"I have to take her to the shrink and then to the Y for swim?" I slammed my dishes into the sink harder than I'd planned.

"Yes, Emily, I need you to drive your mom to appointments, go to the grocery store, and run some errands." Dad slurped his coffee and checked his phone.

"So, I just got my license and now I'm Mom's personal driver?" Wiping my hands on the dishtowel and tossing it on the counter.

"Yes, Emily, we are in the midst of a family crisis." His eyes remained glued to his phone. Apparently, his email was far more important than my life being turned upside down.

"And picking me up. Don't forget me!" Amy chirped like a baby bird in distress.

"Can I use her car? You know, to make her more comfortable," I tried, peeling mom's keys from the hook by the pantry.

What 16-year-old wouldn't want to drive an awesome Lexus SUV?

"Um, no." Dad responded between coffee slurps. "You have a car, Emily."

"Since when does mom swim? She hasn't exercised since her high school PE class and I'm sure she hated it even then. She's always said exercise was a waste of time." I returned mom's keys to their hook, simultaneously ripping mine from where they hung next to it.

"Emily, she wants to get in the water. I think it'll be good for her."

"Because she's a mermaid!? You realize this entire act is ridiculous, right?" I cleared Amy's cereal bowl and spoon from the table and threw them in the sink.

"She was hit on the head, Em. The brain is one of life's biggest mysteries. Just pick her up, please."

"Can't we hit her on the head in the same spot and make her remember us?" Amy asked.

I was glad she said what I have thought since this whole debacle happened. It's not as cute and innocent coming out of my mouth, but Amy's got youth on her side.

"I wish it was that easy, squirt. I'll see you guys tonight. Pizza?" He looked haggard as he stood up and pushed his chair in, still holding his coffee in one hand, the phone in the other.

"Your shirt is wrinkled," I pointed out.

"Yeah, there's a lot going on. Pizza," he said once more.

Pizza did sound good. Why is it that I can be totally bought by bread and cheese?

"Who is watching her while I'm at school?" Panic hit me like a blast of cold air. The thought of leaving my mother home alone all day freaked me out. "Fred's gonna look in on her."

"Fred?!? Our neighbor who is what? 94?"

Dad exhaled a gust of frustration yet again, "Janet will come by for lunch. She should be fine."

"Should?" I took his empty coffee cup from him and added it to the sink. Then why did my stomach feel nervous. Mom didn't remember how to use the phone, let alone the stove. What if she burnt the place down?

"We have fire insurance, right?" I questioned my parent's emergency preparedness, as if they were somehow inept because they hadn't prepared for mom's sudden memory loss. Or amnesia? Or Mermaid-itus. Whatever she suffered from.

Dad waved and ducked into his car, flinging his briefcase onto the back seat.

Amy wanted to say goodbye to Mom before we left, so I followed her to the master bathroom. Mom was in her new favorite place, the bathtub. She wore a one-piece swimsuit and her new leggings. I should have asked dad if we had flood insurance.

"Have a beautiful day! Learn a lot of exciting stuff." She smiled at us and waved like she was in a parade.

It was awkward leaving her, soaking in her sequined leggings, but most teachers don't excuse tardy attendance because your mother rivals the Mad Hatter.

"Goodbye, Mommy." Amy leaned over to kiss her wet head.

"Nora," Mom corrected her. "Nora the Mermaid."

"I'll be here at 3 to pick you up. Don't stay in there all day," I instructed before I bent down and pulled the drain out, tucking it into my backpack. Safety precautions. Just in case. I couldn't explain it, but I didn't feel comfortable leaving my mother in a full tub of water.

Even mermaids can drown.

Amy and I stumbled over boxes as we exited the front door. Piles of Amazon.com boxes were stacked on our welcome mat, all shapes and sizes. A UPS truck was parked on the street, the driver hauling more boxes onto a dolly.

"Christmas in April," joked the driver.

My hand went to my forehead in distress. Nora was online shopping! She couldn't remember us, but she managed to shop with her magic card. Thanks again, Janet.

I had to hurry so that Amy and I wouldn't be late for school, but I shot Dad a text before I started the car.

10,000 boxes on our doorstep. Take the magic card from the mermaid.

It's her money, Emily. She can buy what she wants.

Really? A woman who is convinced she lives in the Pacific Ocean, and is missing her gold-flecked tail, should have liberty to purchase whatever she desires? Shouldn't we be saving her from herself? And I'm the teenager!

Kessia ran out her front door and through Fred's lawn. "Morning, Fred," she shouted as she passed him, cramming papers into her backpack. She continued past Mom's parked Lexus and into my crappy, blue car. I loved being almost next door neighbors with my very best friend.

"Did ya notice how my paint sparkles in the sun?" I asked Kessia, sarcasm slipping off my tongue.

"Don't make fun of her, Emily!" Amy shouted at me.

"Sorry," I exhaled. "Let's just go."

"Um, who barfed in your Cheerios this a.m.?" Kessia asked as she buckled her seatbelt.

We watched as Fred slowly bent down and picked up one of the boxes before Nora greeted him at the door. Together they retrieved the boxes one-by-one.

"Who is watching who?" Kessia looked at me and I could tell she was slightly worried too.

"I'm not sure," I admitted, the worry evident in my voice. "I'm not sure at all."

CHAPTER SEVEN

English was a long, drawn out torture. Mr. Edwards lectured the entire class, oblivious to his nasal drip snorting that occurred every five seconds and grossed us all out. He balanced a pool cue in one hand and a handkerchief in the other like some Shakespearean citing jester. Mr. Edwards explained that he was a nine-ball champion during college and encouraged us to take up the sport. "Billiards teaches strategy and patience," he'd preach, but nobody beyond Stud Muffin Jack ever feigned any interest in his antiquated game.

It wasn't until we were shuffling out of class that José approached me, looking impeccably groomed as always, as if he got a fresh hair cut every morning.

"So, we're doing this English project together," he said. I noticed his mouth pulled to the left when he spoke, most likely a side effect from having a broken jaw. Rumor was that the doctor had squished his face with tongs when he was born and his parents sued the doc's pants off. The malpractice left José with an enormous college fund and a dangerously charming smile.

"Yeah, sorry. Hope that's okay." I didn't know why I was apologizing for an assignment I didn't assign.

"It's cool," he said.

He looked around, probably for someone cooler to talk to. Giving his usual nod to someone who yelled "Yo, José, What up?"

"Oh." I couldn't think of anything to say as we both just stood awkwardly.

"So, tomorrow? Your house?" He smiled at me, giving me his full attention and waited for my response. It was like the clouds parted and the sun was shining only on us. I was going to be alone with the boy of my dreams.

"Sure!" I wanted to spin and sing and dance in place.

He fist-pumped me and took off with his boys, disappearing into the gym. So what if he treated me like one of the guys? I had my first interaction with José and I hadn't fainted. I took it as a positive sign that I would make it through this English project without dying. Definitely a good sign, in my opinion.

Mom was ready and waiting outside on Fred's porch when Amy and I picked her up. Like a gentleman, Fred walked Nora politely to the car and held the door open for her.

"Thank you, Fred!" Nora hugged him.

Apparently, Bart the Pirate had put reminder alarms on mom's cell phone, aka her 'magic thingy,' so she would know what time I was getting her. Nora let me know that they used shells to communicate over long distances underwater. Seriously.

She was wearing new, mermaid scale printed leggings and a t-shirt with textured shells printed on the front. The bag she was carrying had a towel hanging out and Nora explained she had all her swim accessories inside. Okay, so some of the boxes were for her new water sports activities and mermaid attire. I couldn't wait to see what else she had purchased.

We drove to her psychologist while listening to a new playlist, all of which Nora bounced her leg to and marveled at their talent. Nora never listened to music before her accident. She was always on the phone with a client, or co-worker, or with a fellow PTA mom coordinating the next bake sale. She was too busy for music.

Amy and I walked mom into the psychologist office. It was small with a lot of light seeping in the windows, a row of succulents in colorful pots adorned the shelf. A tiny woman in stilettos welcomed us.

"Good afternoon, Nora. I'm Dr. Sy."

"Are we supposed to wait here?" I asked.

"You're welcome to wait in this room. There's magazines or coloring books." She waved her hand out like a game show hostess.

"What? Like with crayons?"

"They are for kids and adults. Teenagers too. People find them very soothing; it's almost meditative. Or there's an ice cream parlor two blocks down. Your mother and I will be fifty minutes."

"Oh, I'm not their mother. Well, not their birth mother. I'm a mermaid," Nora said.

I lifted her t-shirt slightly, exposing the stretch marks on her love handles. The reddish-purple lesions stood out on her pale skin. "See these bad boys? Those are from me."

Mom's face turned bright red and she swatted my hand away, releasing her shirt.

"Some are from me, right!?" Amy asked.

"We will be about fifty minutes," Dr. Sy repeated, leading Nora into her office. "Okay, Nora…tell me about being a mermaid," was the last thing I heard before she closed the door between us.

Amy wanted to color, so we sat on the floor and opened a book of animals, picking a page of dolphins.

"Is everything going to be okay?" She asked me, careful to stay in the lines.

"Yes, of course it is." I said what one is supposed to tell kids when shielding them from life's curve balls. But I asked myself the same question. Was anything ever going to be okay again?

CHAPTER EIGHT

José was inside my house for exactly ninety-five minutes. We went over the outline I started and I think we accomplished a little bit, but I was too distracted by José being in my presence. Everything about him distracted me.

He had his career path all figured out and knew exactly what he was going to do with his life; a mechanical engineer specializing in automotives.

"How did you decide? I'm not even sure about all the options out there. I mean, I know I'll work. But what do I want to do all day?"

"What do you do now?" he asked.

"Besides listen to music and social media?" I answered honestly, though I sounded trivial and juvenile even to my own ears.

"Yeah?" He inquired, forcing me to dig deeper.

"Watch fake reality TV. I'm a shallow mess." The more I talked the worse I sounded. Was I really this superficial? No wonder I had no future plans. "What does Savannah do in her free time? Save orphans? Knit sweaters for dog shelters? Sing to Veterans?" Why was I asking about his girlfriend? Did I want him to know that I knew he was off the market?"She studies science and space mostly," José took a folder out of his backpack.

"A future astronaut. I had no idea." Why would I? It's not like Savannah and I follow each other or have had any contact in the last decade.

"Yeah, she's focused," he threw back, looking for a specific page of notes from Mr. Edwards' class.

Why didn't I want to go into space? Maybe because I watched *The Martian* a few years ago and Matt Damon had to eat potatoes he grew from his own poop fertilizer. Or maybe I had zero ambition. I hated to think that Mom's bestie, Janet, could be right and I was a lazy, mooching cow, destined for nothingness.

I set a reminder on my phone to meet with the school counselor. I wanted to figure out what I was interested in before my peers all left me in the dust. And I had to face the facts; José was in love with Savannah. They'd be Mr. Automotive Mechanical Engineer and Mrs. Astronaut, and I'd be Loser Without Ambition.

José bolted. It was like the eject button was pushed and he flew off the couch and towards the door. His legs looked dangerously good in those basketball shorts.

"Catch ya later," he shouted. It was as personal as a preset text, "I'm busy" or "I'm driving, will return call as soon as I can." José's universe was stratospheres away from mine. We weren't destined to be together after all.

Kessia came over the second José left, dying for details. Again, the benefit of having your best friend live one house over.

"He hates me," I shrugged. "As expected."

I signaled to Amy that she could let mom out of her room since José was gone. We had loaded her up with seaweed packets and I had stopped at the craft store to get gemstones and glue to keep them busy. No way did I want José seeing my mother in all her sparkly fish glory.Amy seemed to get it. At such a young age, she wasn't mortified by mom's behavior yet, she could see how it could affect her if mom paraded around the elementary school in mermaid attire.

"Same time tomorrow?" Amy asked. When I nodded yes, she continued, "We are gonna need more glue. And she wants shells."

So what if I was spending my allowance on shiny objects to occupy mom? It was worth the investment to save my sanity. The last thing I needed was for everyone at school to find out our secret. I didn't want the embarrassment, or the pity.

"I guess your mom can't work," Kessia stated, making herself at home at my vanity, and dipping her finger in my eye shadow. It didn't matter that she was ruining it, my make-up applying skills had never been developed. I couldn't make it through one YouTube tutorial without looking like a sad clown.

"She's on temporary disability. A team of doctors were here asking questions yesterday."

"Do they think she's making it up? Like an act?" She asked while smearing shades of blue across her eyelids.

If Nora was acting, she could get an Academy Award. Or at least a daytime Emmy.

"Maybe. They asked her about work and she couldn't answer any of their questions. When she kept crying about missing her starfish friends they packed up and left."

"Instead of buying a sports car and dating someone half her age, she's imitating 'Ariel.' So, like the female version of a mid-life crisis." Kessia compared my mom to her dad. While I thought the two were wildly different, I didn't want to point out that Nora's breakdown was triggered by a car accident. She was hit on the head, and seemed more in love with my dad than she ever had been. All their bickering had stopped, and they were being nice to each other.

It was weird. But nice.

Nora's magic thingy's alarm chimed, signaling it was time for swim.

"Gotta go," I said. "Gotta chauffeur the fish."

Kessia made fish lips at me while she put on her shoes. "It could be worse, you know. At least she doesn't think she's Cleopatra or a Pokemon...or God."

All of those things would suck, but would they be worse? I wasn't sure.

CHAPTER NINE

The YMCA was recently renovated and it was way nicer than I expected. Not quite a luxurious spa feel, but totally Olympic training worthy. The pool was enormous and inviting.

We were approached by Tia, long dreads wrapped into a twisted bun, wearing a lifeguard swim suit and shorts. She held herself with a strength and beauty I normally don't see in girls my age. Maybe she was older, but just looked really young, with great skin. Her ebony was such a contrast to my ivory, and I found myself awestruck by her beauty.

"This is the mermaid?" Tia's smile was welcoming.

"That's me. Nora." Mom fidgeted awkwardly as if she had ice cubes in her underwear.

"Hi, I'm Emily. Her daughter. She hasn't swum in decades."

"I'm Tia, I'll be her swim coach."

"She's an attorney. Or she was," I said dumbly. "I just meant she hasn't *always* been a mermaid."

"She is one now." She shined that smile on me again before linking arms with my mom. "Let's get wet, Nora."

"I'm not sure how graceful I'll be without my tail," Nora warned.

"Not to worry. Feet are as good as fins," Tia prepped, "You'll see. Humans can be great swimmers too."

"I'm gonna try!" Nora exclaimed.

"You're welcome to join us, Emily," Tia offered, as if swimming with my mermaid mother would be a good thing.

"I have homework," I said. And I'd rather swim in lava. Lava erupting from an active volcano.

"Offer stands. See you in a bit." Tia led Nora to the locker rooms, talking like best girlfriends all the way.

I wished I had Tia's confidence and demeanor, and I really needed to work on my posture. Instead, I pulled out my English project homework. I wanted to get a jump on our outline to impress José.

A few droplets of water landed on my page as I wrote. Nora splashed around in the shallow end "getting used to her legs." It was like watching a really bad dinner theater version of *The Little Mermaid* at Sea World. It would have been less dreadful if there were dolphins or whales doing tricks. Or seals. But it was just my mother carrying on about her magnificent tail and how restrictive her swimsuit was, cutting off her circulation. Apparently, Nora preferred to swim topless like the other mergirls, breasts out and all.

How was Tia keeping a straight face? She didn't even seem to judge Nora like I was.

"You're doing great," she encouraged. "Try kicking your legs one at a time. That's right, okay left, now right."

God, it was embarrassing. I wanted to hide, desperate that none of the parents swimming laps recognized me or my mom. Columbus is a pretty small town; we were likely to run into someone Nora knew. What if someone from mom's work saw her like this? She'd be fired for sure. My mind kept going crazy on what people would think. What if they thought I was crazy too?

When they finished with the swim lesson, Tia escorted Nora into the locker room. I worked on my English project until Nora, back in her mermaid attire, was returned to me.

"She's a natural," Tia announced, as if she believed my mother had just acquired her legs.

"Thank you, Tia," Nora beamed. "I can't wait until my next lesson!"

I thought about how I couldn't stick with anything. I had quit soccer mid-season, to my Dad's horror. I ended my musical pursuits in third grade, quitting guitar after only four lessons. And my dreams of being a gymnast fizzled the first time I stepped on a balance beam.

Nora, the attorney, had transitioned into a mermaid seamlessly, going for it with complete dedication. Why didn't I inherit the same perseverance in my DNA?

CHAPTER TEN

As I navigated from P.E. to Chemistry, the unthinkable happened; Savannah spoke to me. My hair was wet and my face was flush from running the mile. There I was, rushing to class, trying to remember if I had completed my homework and bam.

"José told me about your English project."

I made sure she was talking to me. She hadn't even looked at me since first grade. Her eyes were locked on me like a missile's target. They were deep brown and piercing, outlined by mink lashes that stretched up to her eyebrows.

"Yeah," I responded and kept walking. She managed to keep up with me when I quickened my pace, her long legs creeping effortlessly like a spider.

"We should hang out," she said. "Why did we ever stop in the first place?"

She pretended to think about our past, our story that ended at the Indian Cave State Park a decade ago. Was she actually straining to recollect?

Savannah and I were best friends for exactly two months

during the summer after kindergarten. We were inseparable, living at each other's houses, spending every night together. She even managed to put a temporary wedge between Kessia and I that I'll never forgive myself for allowing.

Savannah joined my family camping trip at the Indian Caves where we explored ancient petroglyphs and went horseback riding. Everything had gone storybook, with campfire stories, hiking, and roasting marshmallows. That is, until Savannah peed. She wet her pants while we were balancing on fallen logs and that was it. She didn't talk to me for the entire car ride home and never spoke to me since.

I had to sit by her in fifth grade for an entire year and she never turned her head to look at me. I couldn't imagine what would have happened if I had been the one to pee. Still, I didn't question why her urinating on herself was somehow my fault, understanding that the friendship had come to a dead end. Instead, I begged Kessia for eternal forgiveness and accepted my fate of never being in the cool crowd.

In junior high, I was glad Savannah ignored me. I witnessed other girls fall in and out of her favor and the results often left scars. She was the queen bee of our community and I was happy to be left out of the game. And besides, she intimidated the beejezus out of me.

"Why did we stop hanging out?" she inquired again as if I were our class historian.

"You peed," I wanted to say, but didn't. If she was going to pretend those soiled shorts never existed, I would too.

"I can't remember."

"Me either! We should. Really soon!" and she floated away with her gaggle of popular groupies.

Maybe this was a friendship do-over. Maybe my partnering with José had upped my social status from invisible to acceptable. Or maybe she knew the truth; I was in love with her boyfriend. She could probably smell it, like a stink bug; I was probably producing a foul odor from my abdomen since I felt threatened and cornered. She sensed my womanly betrayal and she was stating her claim. José was hers. As if I didn't know. We both knew our rank in the social food chain.

CHAPTER ELEVEN

After dropping Amy off at her dance lesson, I went home to pick up Nora for her shrink appointment and swim class. I saw Nora and Fred on Fred's porch, huddled on a wooden bench. I parked on the street between our two houses and walked through Fred's white picket fence gate and into his yard.

"Hey Fred, do you think you could take Nora to her appointments sometime?" I planned ahead, knowing I'd need to be at José's over the next few weeks. Maybe Fred could help me out a bit.

"Don't have my license these days. I'm legally blind." He responded without looking at me.

Nora and Fred continued to give all their attention to a gust of feathers. Was that a chicken? Were my mom and Fred suffocating a defenseless bird?

"What's going on?" I asked, noting there were chickens plucking around the yard.

"She had a zip tie on her ankle. We were cutting it off," Fred explained, placing the chicken gently on the porch. Well, at least they weren't torturing the poor thing.

"Whose chickens?"

"Nora wanted them."

"Aren't they lovely?" Nora sang, not really asking.

"Nora wanted to give them a nice home," he continued. "They lay eggs."

Thanks for that factoid, Fred. "The coyotes will get them," I warned.

"I'm going to bring them in the house at night," Fred confided.

Wait? What? What was happening? All my internal alarms went off at once.

"You can't do that! They poop everywhere. It's totally unsanitary and you'll die of some bird poop disease," I shouted, waving my hands in the air for emphasis.

I didn't want Fred to die. Who would take care of Nora during the day? I didn't really know why I felt hot and angry, but I just wanted to get out of there.

Chickens! I couldn't add taking care of chickens to my day.

"Nora, we're going to be late for your appointment! Let's go now." I huffed towards my car, turning back to make sure she was following. She wasn't.

"Pronto! Let's go," I hollered, stomping my foot.

"I'm not going." Nora faced Fred. "She's hostile. Look what she did to me." Nora held up her mermaid shirt and exposed her stretch marks. "…claws like a lion."

"I did those from *inside* your stomach! That is why they are called *stretch*-marks."

She stood next to Fred, petting a chicken. Not budging.

"I cannot help that I was a big baby! It's not my fault!"

Was I really having this conversation? What alternate universe was I living in? I held my hands on my head to keep my brain from exploding out of it.

How was I going to get through to her when she believes I'm a lion? I took some deep breaths and thought about my options.

None were appealing and I needed to get Nora's mermaid booty into my car.

"Okay, sorry, Nora. I'll be nice." I held up my hand in some kind of salute. "I promise. And Fred, I'll talk to my dad about building a chicken coop."

"That would be swell, Sweetie. But no bother. I don't mind them in the house at night."

I bit my lip and refused to let myself argue with him about chickens pooping on Bab's quilt. Or the feathers and chicken dander flying into his nostrils while he snored. Nope, I bit harder.

"Thanks for watching Nora," I waved and forced a smile as Nora pranced to the passenger side of my car.

"It was my pleasure, Darlin'."

As I drove Mom to her appointment, I kept stealing glances as her. She looked like the same person. Kind of. Was she? Did my dad bring the wrong person home from the hospital? They switch babies all the time. I saw a show on it. I'm so giving birth at home when I'm older. Maybe in the bathtub. Then again, thanks to mom's water escapades, the tub is no longer a peaceful place in my mind.

But I couldn't quit thinking about the chickens. Nora would never have had birds before. She used to say how filthy they were. And smelly. Nothing about her was the same. Nothing at all.

CHAPTER TWELVE

Tia sat with me while my mother changed in the locker room. Her dreads were loose, held away from her face with a colorful headband.

"I taught your mom to braid her hair and pull it into her swim cap. Girl's gotta save those pricey extensions."

I didn't care about her stupid extensions or if they got tangled into a nest on her head and birds laid eggs in it. They were ridiculous and she looked foolish wearing them, like one of those moms who tried desperately to remain looking young. Just because you can fit into your teenager's clothes, does not mean you should wear them. And they tell us to "grow up."

Although my mood was in the toilet, I feel better by simply being near Tia. Just breathing next to her was a pick me up. Her energy was contagious.

"What is it about you? I just…I feel lighter."

"We share neurons. All of us humans. I choose to give off uplifting vibes."

I inhaled again. Was she serious or messing with me?

"What do you choose?" she asked.

"I have a choice?"

She nodded. "You can adjust your mood, ya know. You don't have to be cranky all the time."

I'm so not cranky all the time. Am I?

"It's just weird, ya know. I kind of feel like my mother is in a coma, but walking and talking. Is that even possible? A walking coma?" I didn't expect her to have the answers, but I wanted her input.

"Well, scientific research has proven that people do hear what is going on around them while they are in a coma, so it could be possible to be in a different state. The brain is a perplexing organ that has yet to be fully discovered." She smiled at me and pointed at her own head. "Your mom is still your mom, somewhere in there."

We both looked back at the pool as I thought about what she said. The chlorine smelled stronger today and was giving me a slight headache. Was my mom in a weird kind of coma? Was the real her deep inside trying to come out?

"Science has also noted, mostly by patients' testimony, that people in a coma can feel the energy that you bring into the room. If you're in a bad mood, they can feel it. Or, if you are at peace, it comforts them. You have control of what you bring into the room." She stood up and turned back to me, "Every room."

"Can I ask how old you are?" She seemed way older than me, but her face appeared young.

"Twenty," Tia answered.

"Is it rude to say you seem way older?"

"I'm working towards a doctoral degree in psychology. My major is neuroscience and behavior," She explained, seemingly not bothered in the slightest that I'd implied she had the wisdom of an eighty-year-old woman. "I'm nowhere near being a doctor, but it's pretty safe to say you are experiencing unconventional grief."

"Oh, sounds fancy." I tried to joke, but failed. "What does that even mean?"

"You're suffering from a loss, from losing your mother, but she's physically present. She's just not present in the same regard."

I thought about what she said. Was I grieving? I had so many emotions it was hard to pinpoint exactly what was going on inside me.

"Just know that it's normal. Unconventional grief, that is." She grabbed her clipboard, "I'm going to check on your mom."

"You mean Nora the Mermaid."

"Yes. Watch your neurons." She teased me with a smile and walked away.

Tia would be an amazing doctor. Or psychologist. Whatever she was doing, I couldn't really remember. Again, another person who had their future completely mapped out.

I watched as she met Nora at the pool steps. At least Nora was in good hands with Tia, someone who wanted to help her and get into her head.

Nora was wearing a sleek swim cap, not an extension in sight. The sensible side of old Nora would appreciate Tia saving her hair extension investment.

Tia held Nora up as she wobbled down the steps into the pool, yammering about having sea legs.

"One leg at a time," Tia encouraged.

"Knees are so bendy," Nora explained, holding Tia for dear life.

The hour flew by as I did more research on Shakespeare, wanting to sound smart for José. You'd think by reading Wikipedia that Shakespeare was a pretty laid back dude, writing comedies and chillin' with the theater crowd. So, why was I having such a hard time understanding what he was saying? Even though it was English, it was like an entirely different language.

Feeling bold, I dragged Nora into the grocery store with me on the way home. Since she had her magic card on her, I figured I'd load up on snacks and essentials for Amy and me.

It turned out to be yet another poor choice, or extreme lack of discerning judgment, because Nora had a meltdown by the deli when she saw all the "murdered sea creatures" on display.

"What did they ever do to anybody?" She referred to the lobsters, pre-cooked and ready to be eaten. "Barbaric humans... emptying our oceans."

Up until a few weeks ago, she had been one of those barbaric humans. Her pain was real, and while I wanted to be sympathetic, the same display case that upset her was just making me hungry.

Finally, I had to call Bart the Pirate to meet us when Nora refused to stop slobbering all over the glass barrier and begging Poseidon to save them. Her tears and snot were health hazards according to the grocery store manager. Nora was banned from entering their place of business ever again; Dad soothed my mermaid mother; and I grabbed as many frozen dinners as I could fit in the cart.

Maybe Tia was right, I was experiencing unconventional grief. Glorious food was at my fingertips and yet, I couldn't eat a thing.

CHAPTER THIRTEEN

After tucking Mom and Amy away with sea friendly snacks, sea shells, and a new hot glue gun, José arrived to work on our English project. Our conversation flowed effortlessly and naturally, not forced or sporadic like I had feared.

But then, as José was telling me a riveting story about his last fishing competition, Amy bolted out of her and Mom's hideaway.

"I need twine," she demanded.

"BBQ supplies. Dad uses it to tie rotisserie chickens," I said, shooing her away.

Amy headed into the kitchen and José continued his epic adventure tale, not leaving out any details about the weather or his bait. I held onto his every word, while staring at his perfect lips. My brain kept shouting, *"José is talking to me!"* and since I've been fishing with Dad since birth, I was able to contribute ever so slightly to prove that I could relate to his level of enthusiasm.

Amy returned shortly.

I gave her the look. The look that said, *"Why are you out here when we have a deal? You're supposed to keep mom away and ensure the future of your nieces and nephews."*

"Ice pick."

"Camping supplies. Check the cooler in the garage," I said and returned my full attention to José, not even curious as to why a six-year-old watching a mermaid would need a sharp object.

"So, then what happened?"

But Amy was traipsing back through the living room and caught José's attention. "What grade are you in?" José asked her.

Amy held the ice pick at her side in the way she was taught to carry scissors while walking. "First."

"My niece and nephew are in first grade. Carson Elementary?"

"Yes, that's my school."

In that moment, my sister bond with Amy was cemented. We were now on a Kardashian-Jenner level of loyalty, determined to keep our mother's meltdown away from the most popular family in town. It wasn't just about saving my non-existent social status, now her future reputation was on the line. Our silence spoke volumes. Or maybe I was making something out of nothing, but still, we were being sisterly.

Amy left us, returning to her enormous responsibility of keeping Nora tucked out of sight.

José finished his fishing story, to which we both cracked up so hard we ended holding our sides because we couldn't stop laughing. I can't remember if the story was even that funny, or if I was just stressed about making a good impression, or terrified that Nora would make her debut in mermaid pants and hair extensions, but I laughed, and it felt good. José was much more approachable and human than I had anticipated, and I imagined us being close friends and confidantes. If I couldn't date him because of Savannah, we could at least be friends.

Amy popped back in, a little agitated, but trying to keep her cool, "Lace."

Okay, think, I mentally scanned the house. An old dress?

Halloween costume? Where would she find lace?"Place mats from Gran. Check the pantry."

Amy looked relieved.

"Science project, Amy? The twins are making volcanoes," José made contact with her again. He was so polite.

Amy nodded. I guess you could call Nora a sort of science project. She was being researched by a team of doctors and they were collecting data. Only the last thing Amy or I wanted was any sort of peer review.

"Tiny bells," she danced as if she had to pee. Poor thing was getting stressed out finding Nora's requests.

"Christmas decorations. Green bins in the garage," I shouted, pulling my hair into a ponytail.

Amy screamed out from the garage, "Where?"

I screamed back, taking José by surprise, "Rip them off the reindeer set!" Oops. "Sorry."

"School used to be so much more fun. I loved building things and using my hands. Now we have all these papers to write and junk," he folded his paper into a ninja star, his fingers creating the origami by memory. He'd obviously mastered the art of paper folding.

I got what he was saying though. I missed making things and hands-on learning. Lectures were mind-numbing and taking notes seemed so pointless. Everything is online. With Google we don't even need to memorize anything. But we had a project to do.

"How are we going to string all this Shakespeare info together?" I asked, going over my notes again.

José stared at me blankly, "Honestly, I haven't a clue."

And I fell for him even harder. José didn't understand Shakespeare either. It was as if we were in a foreign country and didn't speak the language, but we had each other.

I didn't ask Amy why she needed all those random supplies while babysitting Nora, but I guess I should have. Hindsight is always so clear. I could see where I made the ultimate mistakes.

First, I fell for José. And second, I didn't keep my mom-fish on a leash.

CHAPTER FOURTEEN

I've read enough Greek mythology to know mere mortals should never upset the gods. Being raised by Nora was like having Athena for a mother. Everything was always about justice and honor. Sometimes I wished she would just tell me I was pretty instead of commenting on my industrious cognitive skills or my deductive reasoning, but not Nora. She wanted her girls to be proud of their minds, their ability to play fair and to master playground politics with integrity. Independence was the goal for her daughters.

In a sense, it worked. I wasn't the vainest of high-schoolers, but I had horrible self-esteem. I rarely felt comfortable in my own skin, wishing I could disappear instead of shine in the spotlight. If life were a play, I'd be in charge of lighting, so I could make it pitch black when necessary and always linger in the shadows. But since high school is like its own Shakespearean tragedy, I was thrown into a starring role.

As I made my way to Mr. Edward's English class, students were pointing at me and smirking. Everyone was in on a private joke, and I was the butt.

I checked to see if I was having a wardrobe malfunction. Nope, all parts covered.

Was Eddy the class clown behind me? Nope, I was alone.

Were they making fish lips at me or was I paranoid?

I ran into class and grabbed onto Kessia. She'd be able to bring me up to speed. Kessia would be able to let me know how I had upset the gods and what kind of offering or sacrifice I'd have to make to redeem myself. With her phone in hand, Kessia showed me the awful truth.

Nora was on Snapchat.

The ramifications of having given Amy an ice pick and twine were now apparent.

Nora's long, colorful extensions dangled around her made up face, adorned by pink-silver lip stain. And she was singing. Loudly.

I covered my eyes to relieve the sting as the video jumped from scene to scene. I couldn't turn away. I had to look, even if it burned my cornea.

Nora was attempting to talk to the fish in an aquarium at the pet store, and that wasn't the worst of it. She was wearing a homemade shell bra, the lace placemat Gran had given us sewn to the bottom, barely covering her muffin top. Two massive shells were glued onto the nude bra, covering her breasts. Smaller shells, starfish, and silver Christmas bells were scattered around the base of the bra, swaying and jingling.

Nora spoke to the goldfish as if she knew them.

"Hello, little guys! I miss swimming with you," Nora half spoke, half sang. "Hello, my little friends. It's me, Nora the Mermaid!"

The story cut to Fred, smiling with full dentures showing. "She is a mermaid, all rightly."

So, Nora and Fred had taken a field trip to the pet store.

I was mortified. "Who?" I barely got out. "Why?" I said or thought.

Embarrassment flowed through my veins, making my heart

beat dangerously fast. My hands and feet tingled and I thought I might pass out.

Kessia helped me into my seat and mouthed the one person I knew not to tempt my fate with, "Savannah."

Why was this happening to me? Why did my normally super normal mother go off the deep end and publicly humiliate me?

"It'll be okay," Kessia pacified me like only a bestie can. But we both knew the unspoken truth. I was never, never, never going to live this down.

CHAPTER FIFTEEN

"At least I got her to wear the bra," Amy defended herself. "She wanted to string the twine through the shells. It could have been way worse."

So that was the reason for the ice pick. Shell holes. I hugged Amy. None of this was her fault. I wasn't going to throw our newly formed sisterhood loyalty out the window because of one mishap. I had just lost my mother to blunt force trauma. I wasn't going to lose her too.

"We'll figure it out," I said as much to comfort myself as Amy.

"You sent me to school with a frozen chicken pot pie."

"Sorry."

"Just get Lunchables. And goldfish." She caught herself. "No goldfish!"

News of Nora's mermaid transformation had spread like wild fire, jumping from family to family, the wind fanning the flames. It was a serious hot topic in our small town. It's not every day that one of our own goes completely bonkers.

Our doorbell hadn't stopped ringing all evening. People brought casseroles and muffins.

"We missed your mother at the PTA Meeting," one woman said, handing over banana bread.

"Wish your mom well for us," said a man, handing me his business card that read *Meals on Wheels*. "Let me know if you'd like to take her place for a day. We could always use the help."

One family tried to see behind me to get a view of Nora the Mermaid. Another told me they were "so sorry for my loss."

"She's not dead," I slammed the door. My mother had become a freak show in which everyone wanted a front row ticket.

Dad loaded up on dried seaweed at Costco and asked Janet to help with mermaid friendly meals while he worked late. Apparently, tapioca beads reminded Nora of clam pearls, so she ate pudding by the bowlful. She also took to chia seeds in lime water and acai berries. My mom was not only a mermaid; she was on some sort of supermodel diet with foods I had never heard of. I just wanted a burger or comfort food, but our kitchen was now vegan. Even eggs made her cry, "They're baby chicks!" Somehow she remembered chicken babies, but not her own.

"It will be old news by tomorrow," Janet commented, as if anyone at school would forget mom's makeshift shell bra. Ever. "Mostly people are just worried about themselves, Emily."

This was not going to blow over quickly. José would most likely want a new English partner. Kessia would seek new friendships. I could feel the social quicksand was swirling around me, swallowing me whole.

"Janet, do you know how many mermaids are in the Pacific Ocean?" Amy asked, "Are they in pods, or do they live by themselves?"

"I'm not a mermaid expert, Kiddo." Even Janet treated Amy like she was younger than she was.

"The answer is zero, Amy. Zero mermaids live in the Pacific Ocean because they do not exist," I said, annoyed that I was the only one being honest.

"It's dark in the deep parts of the ocean, right? So, how does she see down there?" Amy asked, refusing to listen to the truth. It was as if she wanted our mother to be a mermaid. Maybe she thought she'd be a mermaid too. It was so frustrating and I had to stop the nonsense.

"She doesn't!" I yelled. "No one can see in the bottom on the ocean. There's no electricity down there. No lights." My hands shot up in the air again because somehow that made my point more effective, more true.

Dad entered through the back door, just in time to hear me yelling at my sister. I hated when he caught me being a jerk without the proper context. As if the context would make me appear less jerky.

"Emily, that's enough," Dad barked. He collected himself and sat back down at the table. "Your sister is just trying to make sense of your mother's condition. We are all just trying to figure this out."

Amy took this as her cue to continue, "So, are there different mermaid races? Or are all mermaids Caucasian?"

"Oh. My. God. Please make her stop!" I covered my face with my hands, maybe that would help make this all go away. If I didn't see it, it wasn't happening, but I didn't have extra hands to cover my ears. I could still hear the mayhem.

"Is everything okay?" Nora came in from her bath, fresh glitter on her cheeks and pounds of blue eye shadow. Was that a new shell crown?

My mother wore a massive amount of shells and gems on her head like she was queen of the sea. The gemstones sparkled in the kitchen light, ricocheting rainbows on the walls and countertop. She had to hold her neck straight and sit down slowly in order to keep her makeshift crown from falling off her head.

"Please don't fight." She joined us at the table, petting Amy's hair and smiling adoringly at my father.

"We're not fighting, Nora. We're all good," Dad shot me a stern look.

"Good," Nora sat down with us. "There is no fighting under the sea. No arguments even. Everyone just loves each other. Right, Bart," she looked to my father for confirmation.

"That's right, Nora." Janet chimed in, stirring some sort of vegan concoction on the stove like an urban witch. I couldn't comprehend why everyone continued this façade. It was as if they were working to keep my mother's memory from returning. Why didn't they want my real mother to return?

"Your crown is so beautiful!" Amy beamed. "The starfish are my favorite, and the purple stones. Those are my other favorite."

"It is beautiful, Nora," Dad added and something inside me snapped.

"Quit enabling her!" I shouted. "You are not a pirate. She is not a mermaid. This is ridiculous! That crown is obnoxious! I'm losing my mind now!"

Nora's mouth dropped in horror, "You're not a pirate?"

"Of course I am," Bart appeased her.

"You lied to me?" Nora questioned him, shrinking like a scared child. She held onto her shell crown as she backed away from the table. It was crushing to see my mother so distorted and frightened. She used to be so strong and fearless, ready to take on the world.

I could feel Janet's death stare. She'd probably put a curse on me with her vegan voodoo, or poison me. Amy started to cry and Dad covered his face with his hands.

I vowed in that moment to prove to Nora she was our mother. I would figure out a way to make her remember. I'd build a case so strong, with mountains of evidence, there would be no denying the facts.

Nora asked again, barely above a whisper, "Are you a pirate?"

"He's a pirate," I announced, trying to sound convincing, but lacking any enthusiasm. I didn't want to enable my mother, but I didn't want to hurt her either, and now I was on a mission. I'd prove Nora is our mother and everything would be normal again. I'd let her have a little more time believing she's a mermaid while I built my case, and yes, I'd let her believe that dad is a pirate for now. "Bart is a pirate. The best pirate ever."

CHAPTER SIXTEEN

J osé and I sat at our kitchen table, our homework scattered all over it, and oozing onto the chairs. I didn't worry about Amy hiding Nora since surely José knew about her recent fish revelation. I was going to let that pink elephant dance around the room and sit on my lap. There was no way I was going to board that crazy train with José.

José looked up from his work, turning to me. "You know, once a secret is public it loses its power over you."

Did José just go all Yoda on me? I just looked at him, seriously not getting what he was saying.

"Secrets are hard to keep. They weigh you down," he continued.

"I'm embarrassed," came shooting out my mouth before I could stop myself. "Like my mom threw herself a beauty pageant...and then crowned herself the winner. She wears a crown. Like she's a queen or something. It's bonkers!"

It was all too much. Even I couldn't figure out where my anger stopped and my grief started. I was a blubbering mess on the inside, and now on the outside too. I hoped snot wasn't running down my face.

"I have a secret," José looked in my eyes.

It was intense. Like something I'd only seen in movies. Was José going to confess his secret to me? Was I supposed to bless him like a priest? Would I be able to tell Kessia the secret or would I be sworn to secrecy?

"Savannah and I aren't really a couple," he stated matter-of-fact as if he were reading a teleprompter on the six-o-clock news.

My face showed my confusion, my eyebrows scrunched together and my lips ducked out.

"Our parents want us to be together," José said, twisting his hands together.

"Like an arranged marriage?" I clarified.

"Sort of. Yes."

"But she's your girlfriend?" I asked, feeling a spark of hope. A tiny, but powerful spark that ignited like a match.

"Yes and no."

The spark flickered, ready to be snuffed out if needed. I would not give myself false hope.

He sat back in the couch and exhaled the weight of the universe from his chest, then began telling his story starting with the fact that their mothers had gotten pregnant at the same time on purpose so their kids could be best friends, only José was a boy and Savannah was a girl so their dreams of BFF charm bracelets and matching dresses were trampled. They also scorched my delusional dreams of doing the exact same thing with Kessia in the future. Now that I had perspective, it was super creepy and not natural to coordinate gestations.

"So, we did start to date, and I liked her. She was fun and pretty and we liked to fish," he looked down. "But then they kept showing us these pictures of us in the bathtub together as toddlers and it just…"

"Was just?" Again, did I want to hear his answer? That spark in my heart was growing and I was getting less and less able to control it.

"Gross," he finished. "She's like my sister."

My mind was spinning, trying to comprehend. Why was José pretending to be with Savannah? Was José just tricking me to feel my boobs? I didn't have big ones like Savannah. Was I hallucinating?

"I'm glad I could tell you." His smile slowly spread to swoon worthy status.

"Me too," I fumbled with my words. "I mean, I'm glad too. Really glad. I think. Wait, did you say you're not with Savannah? I heard that correctly?"

"Savannah is not my girlfriend," He looked directly in my eyes again.

I had absolutely no idea if he liked me or if we were now girl/boy besties. But didn't he just say that Savannah was his girl bestie. No, she was like his sister. Crap, I should have taken notes. My brain worked best when I wrote things down. It was my way of keeping my mental files organized.

José was not with Savannah!

Later tucked into my bed, the covers pulled up to my neck, I tried but couldn't sleep no matter how many sheep I counted, or breathing exercises I performed, or any of the other sleep antics I found online. Everything José told me kept replaying in my head, as if on automatic loop. He wasn't really with Savannah. I had a shot at getting the guy and living happily ever after. It wasn't much, but even the possibility kept me up all night.

CHAPTER SEVENTEEN

Nora seemed distressed when I picked her up from the shrink, but her mood improved upon greeting Tia.

"You should swim with us." Tia said, folding her arms.

"Can't, have too much homework," I used my usual excuse. Though the water was inviting, I just couldn't make myself indulge Nora.

"Nora, I'll catch up to you in a minute. Why don't you go change?" Tia suggested. We both watched my mom prance all the way into the women's locker room. I still was not used to the prancing. "Emily, I'm concerned about Nora."

"Yeah, aren't we all?" She's been dressed like a mermaid for almost three weeks.

"She asked me the quickest way to the Pacific Ocean. I think she's a flight risk."

"What do you mean?" Panic bungee jumped down my windpipe and sprung up and down in my lungs. It was hard to breathe, let alone talk. "Flight risk?"

"Your family might want to consider a facility that is able to watch her. If she gets on a bus or train it could be a more serious situation. I'm sorry to alarm you and I've left two messages for your father, I just thought you needed to know. Nora believes her home is on the other side of California. At some point, she may just go." She placed a hand on my shoulder. "Do you need my help finding a place, Emily?"

I shook my head no. No, this seemed like something my dad needed to do. Something we needed to talk about. Explore. We couldn't just lock my mother away, could we? It seemed wrong and sad and scary all at once.

"Okay, I'm going to check on Nora." Tia gave me a sympathetic smile before leaving me with my thoughts.

I had to figure out how to prove to Nora she wasn't a mermaid.

I took out a new notebook and thought about how I could convince Nora that she was my mother. The entire stretch marks fiasco had backfired on me, so I knew that I had to not only gather evidence, I'd have to work on how I presented it to her. Being our mother had to be demonstrated without a reasonable doubt and presented in a way that Nora would no longer want to be a mermaid. It was going to be tricky.

First, I'd gather all the family photos, but so far no pictures hanging on the wall had triggered any recollection. I'd have to contact Gran about the birth video she had hidden away, allegedly videoed without mom's consent. Gran has always claimed she was just capturing a precious moment, but Nora has insisted on several occasions that Gran destroy said video since it was a violation of her privacy rights, and mine I guess. Maybe I could give Gran my consent and use the birth video as part of my evidence. I'd have to watch it first to make sure it didn't traumatize mom any further.

Mom's swimming had improved immensely and distracted me from my list. She no longer floundered around and now actually moved effortlessly through the water. Tia taught her to flip and kick off the wall in order to continue her laps. It was like watching fish in a tank. I was mesmerized. And upset. Why did my mother want to leave us so badly?

What's up? A text from José arrived.

Holy crap, my life had changed. José was texting me. Me!

Doing homework, I started and then deleted it.

Chilling, I wrote, and then deleted that too.

At my mom's swim class, doing homework. You? I sent it.

Homework too. He responded.

I waited. Was that it? Was he going to send anything else? Was I supposed to respond? I wish I could ask Kessia all these vital questions.

I saw this. Thought of you. He sent with an attachment.

I opened the link, discovering a Teen Scene Quiz, *"What YOU are Meant to DO."*

I started the quiz immediately, mom's case would have to wait. Suddenly, Nora escaping across the country to be with her merpeople didn't faze me. A quiz José sent became the most important thing in the world. He was taking an interest in me and my future. Maybe we were destined to be together after all.

What do you want your boyfriend to buy you for Christmas? With choices a) A diamond ring b) A microscope c) A kitten d) what boyfriend?

Did José read this already and know what the results would be? Was I supposed to answer the questions as if José was my boyfriend? It was way too premature for that. He just told me he wasn't with Savannah. Why was a Quiz about my career asking a question like this? Again, Kessia would know what to do here.

I chose b) the microscope by deduction. A diamond ring would make me look materialistic, a kitten would make me appear needy, and I wasn't about to send a signal that I wasn't interested in José, which I was. Very.

After filling out five more questions about my lipstick preferences and which side I sleep on, the results were in. Teen Scene had determined that I was meant to be an Endocrinologist. Why? Because they use microscopes to test blood and tissue samples. What did that have to do with my lipstick?

A doctor. Endocrinologist. I texted.

Impressive.

I pass out when I see needles. Probably not good if a doctor can't see blood.

The search continues. We'll figure it out. He sent back.

José was offering to help me discover my life goals!? Did this mean he liked me? Or was I flying in friend zone?

"She's all yours," Tia announced. Nora hugged her goodbye.

I tucked my phone away, unable to stop smiling. I'd talk to dad about Nora's California dreams, but not even Nora the Mermaid could ruin my good mood.

CHAPTER EIGHTEEN

Nora paced the living room, chewing on one of her jeweled nails. Her hair extensions fluttered around her face.

"He doesn't talk like a pirate."

I could hear her thinking out loud. I had planted the seeds of doubt and they were as powerful and insidious as an ad campaign.

"He doesn't say Matey."

"Bart is a pirate," I shouted over to her. All I wanted to do was finish my history homework and she was babbling like a maniac. To keep my mother complacent, I lied. If it pleased her, he could be the one pirate in Nebraska.

"He doesn't have a McCaw."

"Pirates have parrots," I argued pointlessly, as we didn't have either type of bird.

"No wooden leg," she continued.

The always helpful Amy chimed in, "Or a hook!" Whose team was she on?

"Okay you two. Not all pirates have wooden legs or hooks. In fact, most pirates don't. Now, we all know that Bart is a pirate. So let's get our homework done and then I'll start dinner."

I texted Dad: *Mom doesn't think your pirate-y enough.*

Since he didn't respond, I took it a step further.

Perhaps an ear-piercing and some tattoos would convince her.

Thanks, Matey, he sent and I laughed. When did my life get so weird?

"WE NEED TO FEED THE GOAT," Nora said.

"What goat?" I asked.

"At Fred's," Amy clued me in.

I grabbed a flashlight and we travelled next door together. Kessia was sitting on Fred's porch steps, petting a goat. "How cute is she?"

Cute? Yes, but why another animal?

Fred answered from inside the new chicken coup on his porch. "Hey, Em. Hi there, Amy. I'm just giving the girls some blankets."

"They have feathers, Fred." This man knew nothing about chickens, and now he had a goat.

"She's the sweetest thing ever," Kessia cooed. As an avid animal lover, this was a dream come true for her, she was oblivious to the goat eating her shoestring.

Dread planted itself in my stomach, churning acid and making me queasy. I didn't have time to take care of chickens and a goat, and Amy, and drive Nora all around town. I had too much homework. I had to figure out what to do with José. And I had to prove to my mother that she actually was my mother. This was all overwhelming.

"Okay, Amy, we need to get inside," I scooted Amy and Nora back towards our house. "See ya, K."

"Night, Em. Happy José dreams," she snickered.

"Come on, Nora." I cajoled her gently. "Bart the Pirate

should be home soon. Maybe you need to primp or something to look good for him."

I couldn't wait to tell dad I had gotten some protein in Nora, even if it was tofu. Since this whole thing happened she's been dropping weight at what had to be an unhealthy speed. It wasn't that she was obese, but she had some cushion on her and back fat around her bra straps. Now her face was starting to look gaunt and her stomach was almost down to the pre-baby era I'd only seen in photos.

But Dad didn't come home until after midnight so I still hadn't talked to him about Nora's desire to return to the Pacific Ocean. And since my father wasn't being pirate-y enough, I spent hours placating my mermaid mother with YouTube videos of ink squirting octopi and deep sea dives. Then, I soothed Nora to sleep with the first installment of *Pirates of the Caribbean*, fast forwarding through all the bad parts because in her fragile head pirates were sweethearts, not thieves.

"…but they're pirates," I said, not getting the appeal. Well, I do get it. Johnny Depp and all.

"They're sensitive," she winked at me. "And sexy."

She was right. I wouldn't mind being lost at sea with José and I would gladly be his wench. Unless wench means prostitute, then I'd just be a girl pirate.

CHAPTER NINETEEN

"Don't forget, you're picking up your mother from swim at three," Dad's voice startled me as I poured a heaping cup of coffee.

How could I forget? My life had become driving Nora the Mermaid to swim lessons and Dr. Sy's office. If I had one of those self-driving cars they would automatically drive to those two destinations. Shrink and swim. Swim and shrink.

Dad had been completely opposed to putting mom into a facility. He had a talk with Fred about keeping tabs on mom and was convinced she would stick around for the animals her and Fred kept adopting. Bart the Pirate seemed to completely miss the fact that my own mother would stay in Nebraska for poultry, but not her daughters. Seemed perfectly legit.

"We are a family in crisis, Emily," He reiterated. "I need you to step up for the time being. We have to keep your mother..."

"Nora the Mermaid," I reminded him since he was stating the obvious to me again.

"Yes, Nora the Mermaid. We need to keep her happy and here, in Nebraska. At home with the people who love her."

"Amy sure does." I smirked. Off his look, "I do, too. I'm on it. You can count on me, Dad. Everything is completely under control."

But honestly, I was freaking out about how I was going to go to José's to work on our project. Canceling the time I had scheduled with José was not an option. Amy was going to a friend's house until Dad got off work, so I just had to make sure Nora was taken care of. The absolute only person I could trust was Kessia, who swore she would get my mom home safely before seven.

Kessia drove my car and dropped me off in front of José's house.

"You sure you're good with this?" I asked again before opening the car door. It felt weird to be in the passenger seat of my own car.

"Yes, don't worry." Kessia adjusted the rear view mirror and then shooed me with her hands. "Go!"

"You're not going to sell photos of her to National Geographic or anything crazy, right?" I couldn't calm the bees buzzing in my gut.

"She's not a *real* mermaid...or I so would."

Kessia was a born entrepreneur. She used to sell smelly markers during elementary school. The popular scents like root beer and grape could cost up to a dollar each, while the cherry sold for a quarter because it reminded everyone of cough syrup. It took Kessia's parents three years of purchasing marker sets before they realized their daughter had turned her school supplies into a business.

"Please don't do anything that will get me in trouble."

"Scouts honor," she said, while flashing me the peace sign.

"And don't let her out of your sight!"

My heart leapt into my throat as she drove off in my car to pick up my mother. Every warning signal flashed in my brain. Kessia got her license before me, but her single mom didn't have the funds to purchase a car. As I watched her run a stop sign while making a sharp right, I wondered if this was such a good idea.

Was Kessia responsible enough to babysit my mom?

CHAPTER TWENTY

"You okay?" José greeted me on his perfectly manicured lawn.

"Yeah," I smiled. I was okay now that he was in front of me. My insides got all mushy and every thought of Kessia and Nora the Mermaid slipped peacefully from my mind.

We went inside and he gave me the quick tour of the downstairs of his house. It was like stepping into a catalog or a makeover show on HGTV, a combination of homey and staged, as if a photo shoot would happen at any moment.

"Your place is so perfect."

"Yeah, my mom's obsession is our home." He grabbed us two lemonades from the fridge.

"My mom works so much; she doesn't have a lot of time for home stuff." Or, at least she used to be that way. I shrugged awkwardly, knowing that now my mom had a different excuse for not being a pinup model for HGTV.

"She will again," he said confidently, as if he knew about mermaid maladies. I hoped he was right. His presence was so strong, so sure. I wanted to crawl into his t-shirt and have his big arms wrapped around me for all eternity.

Amelia, José's mom, arrived like a firecracker, dropping loads of bags onto the table, her arms flying as she spoke a mile a minute. Her brown hair bounced around her face, her gold hoops dangling, trying to keep up with their owner.

"Welcome. Emily, Right?"

"Yes, thanks."

"English project, right?" Amelia rolled her eyes. "Why do they still make you guys learn that Shakespeare junk? Useless. Kids need to learn skills they will actually use. Things that are important like science. Mechanics. Plumbing. We will always need plumbers."

"Yeah, plumbers," I agreed.

"Every single person poops," she stated the undisputed fact. "Robots won't replace plumbers."

I had never thought about the longevity of a plumbing career, or which jobs robots would replace.

"We will need robot fixers. Robots will break down, like cars, and real, live people are going to have to fix them. Is there robot mechanics at school? No, it's Shakespeare from a million years ago. What does that teach you? Nothing."

"Computers are the future," she finished. "And robots."

"So, the project," José said, ushering me from his mom.

"The project," I confirmed, relieved to get away from Amelia, and thankful that I didn't ask her about the possibility of robot plumbers. I didn't want to waste my sacred time with José listening to his mom rant about poop and technology.

José led me to a room adjacent to the dining room, a hide-away best described as a man cave. Oak wood, fishing trophies, and a poker table reeked of testosterone.

"My dad basically lives in here after work. He only comes out when he smells food."

We slid onto a comfy couch in front of a monstrous TV that probably hadn't projected anything but sports.

"I found some videos explaining Shakespeare in modern English. Thought it might help."

I grinned. Having Shakespeare translated so that I could actually understand it would be a game changer. At least I wouldn't feel as stupid.

José's fingers pressed buttons on a digital remote and a video started. Some high school age students reenacted a scene, halting in the middle to ask, "Hold up, what is this guy even saying?"

We laughed as they expressed their own struggle to understand Elizabethan speak before launching into slightly outdated, but totally understandable slang.

He took my hand, interlacing his fingers. "You cold?"

We watched another scene play out, but I couldn't even think about what the high school students were saying. José's hand in mine had completely turned off all comprehensible thoughts. And then he pulled a faux fur blanket around us. It was like being covered in the softest bunnies, and before I knew it we were kissing. José Hernandez had his tongue inside my mouth. I was dizzy with love and lust and raging hormones.

And he kissed me again. Even though everyone believed he was with Savannah. Even though his mother was in the other room, most likely thinking about robots. And I absorbed every wonderful second of it.

CHAPTER TWENTY-ONE

José sprawled out on the grass while I stepped up and down on the curb, my arm on his mailbox. My nerves were tingling and my heart was pounding in my chest. Kessia was exactly eleven minutes late.

"Should I text again?" I asked.

"Not while she's driving. She'll be here."

He reminded me of the no texting and driving contract I'd signed the morning before my mom's accident. I had never really thought about what would happen if I broke one of our contracts, taking them as law and never doubting their power. What if I had written on the walls, breaking our "crayon rules" contract? Or if Amy broke her commitment to being a Brownie and then Girl Scout Contract? Would Nora take us to family court? Did Juvenile Detention Centers honor parent drawn contracts? Would I have a permanent record?

It dawned on me that the contracts were worthless. Without Nora to oversee and enforce our family rules, what was the point? Or maybe the contracts were pointless after all.

José played with a blade of grass, whistling with it between his hands. How was he always so cool? How did he make me so un-cool? We had kissed and groped like boyfriend and girl-friend, but I couldn't shake the reality that he was make-believe with Savannah. I didn't know what to think. Or do. And Kessia being late was solidifying my fear that I'd be the only sophomore in our high school to die of a heart attack without strenuous exercise or drinking 5-hour caffeine drinks.

My car came screeching around the corner and stopped three houses down. Did Kessia not see us waiting for her? José and I walked to an oblivious Kessia and Nora deep in conversation.

"But how do mermaids actually do it? Like humans? Because I don't see any boy or girl parts, just fish scales." Kessia asked.

The last thing I wanted was José to listen to Kessia and Nora discussing mermaid anatomy and reproductive practices.

"You're late!" I interrupted.

"Sorry about that, our appointment ran over."

Kessia got out of the car and moved to get in the back seat. That's when I saw her new hair; identical to Nora's. Colorful extensions dancing as she moved. My best friend was a mermaid too!

"Good night, Ladies," José bowed and ducked back towards his house. I still couldn't believe that gorgeous set of lips had been pressed against mine.

I waited until he was out of earshot and I was inside the car before exploding. As I drove off, I railed into Kessia.

"I can't believe you."

She puffed up her new mane. "When would I ever get the chance to have rainbow braids?"

"You took advantage of a sick person." I hoped I sounded stern.

"It was her idea!" Kessia pouted.

"Doesn't she look wonderful? Emily, we can take you to an appointment too!" Nora added from the back seat.

I gave Kessia a look at the red light. A look that said, "I can't believe you betrayed me."

"Hey, I'm sorry. I was with a mermaid and a magical credit card. I'm weak." She batted her eyelashes at me and pouted

"Kessia, what if it's like this?" I motioned to Nora in the backseat, "Forever? You didn't think it would last a week, and... well? Any signs of...her?"

She bit her lip and shook her head no. "Sorry, Em. I guess I just really thought it was an act."

"Yeah. It's not. I'm not sure what to do, but I'm building a case. I ordered a DNA kit. I'm gathering evidence..."

Nora interrupted from the backseat, "Let's build sandcastles!"

Kessia and I looked at each other, silently confirming we'd talk about it when Nora was not in the car with us.

"So, how was it?!?" Kessia asked, twisting her new hair in her fingers and pretending to be coy. "You spent an afternoon at the man of your dreams house. Dish!"

We are going to live happily ever after and make beautiful babies. His lips are softer than clouds and taste like cherries and I know this because José Hernandez, the love of my life, kissed me, I thought, but knew I couldn't say.

"Good. Nothing to report, really."

It was the first time I had a secret from her and it felt dirty and illicit. And like I had found the pot of gold at the end of the rainbow, but couldn't share any of my magical coins.

We pulled into my driveway, and thankfully Dad was not there yet. He'd be blissfully unaware that I'd negated my mermaid watching duties to Kessia, who had taken advantage of my mother's mermaid delusion to get herself colorful hair extensions. Ugh, why was teenage life so incredibly complicated?

Kessia bounced out of the car, swishing her new hair around obnoxiously, completely oblivious to the I-heart-José fiesta playing in my mind. When we finally came out as a couple in public, I wanted a real party…with a piñata.

"You can't come over?" I asked.

"Nah, Jack's on his way. We've got a ton of work to do. Haven't barely started."

"Stud Muffin Jack is coming?" I whistled for effect.

As if on cue, a monster truck turned the corner and headed towards us. Music booming so loud the ground thumped. The truck parked in front of Kessia's house and shook like a dog as it settled.

"Don't fall in love." I heckled.

She turned again as she reached Fred's yard, "I won't! Let me know when I can watch her again!"

She had her heart safely tucked away, still bruised from her dad's infidelity. A part of me was jealous that she was able to turn off her emotions. Unlike Kessia, my heart was hanging out in the open by a cliff, and I knew I was playing dangerously close to the edge.

CHAPTER TWENTY-TWO

I thought about José constantly. It was like he planted a brain eating amoeba into my head that was taking over. It was pure torture to witness him and Savannah at school; their groups of friends co-mingling, while I sat on the sidelines. Sometimes he'd wink at me, or send me a sly, knowing grin, but I didn't like being his secret, like I was somehow defective.

Savannah floated around me like a butterfly, "How's your mom?"

"Same." I held my books up closer to my chest, hoping they'd be as solid as Kevlar if Savannah decided to take me out. Paranoia snuck into my mind and took over.

"Do the doctor's think she's going to get better?" Savannah asked, placing a hand on my shoulder.

"Not sure."

Why was Savannah talking to me? I wanted to go back to the last ten years when she pretended I didn't exist. Being on Savannah's radar made me uncomfortable. And I couldn't even be mad at her since I was the one sneaking around with her boyfriend.

Uck. I'd make the worst criminal. I'd turn myself in. The guilt was deadening my soul.

"We should grab a coffee," Savannah said, dropping her hand from my shoulder.

As if it was a good idea for me to be alone in public with Savannah. I'd be surrounded by the cool kids as they poured hot coffee in my eyes and ears until I confessed to being madly in love with Savannah's boyfriend..

"Sounds fun," I lied, making a mental note to start walking around the campus to get to my classes and avoid Savannah's wrath. There was no way on earth I was meeting her for a coffee, or for anything.

"C-ya," she swiveled away as I caught my breath.

My phone buzzed in my pocket, waking me from my Savannah-is-going-to-kill-me trance.

Meet me by the bleachers, José texted.

I looked around to make sure nobody was paying attention and slipped off towards the football field. Everyone seemed to be heading to their next class as we had three minutes before the bell. I ducked around the lockers and across the open space to where José was waiting.

"Hi."

"Hey."

He swooped in for a hug. We held onto each other as the bell rung. I was officially late for P.E., but I was in his arms, so everything was okay.

"The coaches will be out soon," I warned.

"Yeah, want to get out of here?"

As if I could say no to that grin. I nodded.

We grabbed each other's hands and headed to the parking lot. I could hear Coach Peter's whistle blowing as I scrambled into José's truck. I had never ditched class before, and it felt both good and strange. And illegal.

"Where are we going?" I didn't care, but asked anyway. The

truck roared to life as I ran my hands over the worn, cracked leather.

"Food. I need sustenance," he looked at me and then back at the road, stealing glances every few seconds. My insides purred a deep contentment; my cells were carbonated. Though held securely by the seatbelt, I was floating.

Lula's Taco's was only five minutes away and the parking lot was empty.

A homeless man talked to himself on a bench by the curb. "My wife thinks we should vacation in the Bahamas, but Jesus saves us…the van braked wrecked, five. Five. Five." He rambled on nonsensically, his arms wrapped in scarves like a colorful mummy. His speech grew louder, more maniacal. The scent of body odor and urine invaded my nostrils and brought bile to my throat. Instinctively, I moved closer to José for protection.

José did the universal sign for crazy with his finger by his head and protectively steered me around the bench. The homeless man jolted towards us.

"Whoa, Dude. Back off!" José held his hand out, pushing the man back onto the bench. "Check yourself."

The homeless man realized he was sitting on the Realtor's face, which read, Donna Martinez, #1 Realtor in Columbus Seven Years Straight, with her phone number underneath. "My wife. My wife. I'm sorry, Sweetie." He scooted over so that he was sitting next to her painted on smile, perfect hair, and sparkly white teeth. He rocked as he profusely apologized to the picture on the bench.

"What a nut job," José announced as he guided me into Lula's. "You okay?"

"I guess," I said. But I wasn't. That guy had scared me. He could have hurt us. He thought the realtor's picture was his wife. And he reminded me too much of my mother. I shuddered.

People were suffering worse than Nora. My mother's delusion had her in a happy, make believe world of sparkles and songs. This man's mind had taken him to a dark place. He needed help and I didn't know how to help him. I didn't know how to help my own mother.

"You sure you're okay?" José nudged me.

I wasn't. Yes, even before my mother's incident, I knew there was a homeless problem, but I always thought it was their fault and that they were drug addicts. Now it wasn't so clear. I had so much to learn about mental illness and I didn't even know where to begin. I couldn't explain to José how I was feeling because I was still figuring it out myself.

I shook it off, hoping my mother's genetic test would arrive soon so I could continue gathering proof. I had ordered the DNA kit as part of my case I was building and if anything would awaken the attorney inside her it was facts. And maybe expert witnesses.

We grabbed a seat by the door and ordered tacos and cokes.

"Do you skip class a lot?" I asked.

"No, just when it's an emergency."

"Where's the fire?" I joked.

"I saw Savannah talking to you. I wanted to make sure we were cool." His foot found my legs, wedging its way between my knees. It was both awkward and nice all at the same time.

Were we okay? Was I?

"Yeah." I said, not wanting to think so much.

There hadn't been enough time to show him my insecurities. It wasn't like José and I were serious. I couldn't start giving ultimatums or nagging him before our relationship even started. So, I switched the subject.

"I met with the school counselor. She had me take all these personality tests and stuff."

"Yeah, what was the verdict?"

"Everything that I'm interested in will put me into poverty. I'm not sure I'd be happy if I were unable to pay for things like electricity. Wi-Fi and all."

"Marry well. I hear mechanical engineers do okay."

Yes. Yes, I will marry you right now, I thought, but didn't want to appear easy.

"With skyrocketing divorce rates, I'll need a career safety net," I challenged and his foot dropped from between my knees. Had I gone too far? Or was his foot heavy?

"Is that so?" He raised his eyebrows.

"And a rock solid pre-nup." I was only half joking and not about to back down. A girl's got to protect herself these days. Nora had told Amy and I since birth that we had to be able to take care of ourselves. "Be a partnership," she coached, "not a second mortgage." I never really thought about what she meant, but it had somehow sunk in. Nora didn't want Amy or me to end up divorced and reliant on an ex-spouse. Was Nora planning to divorce my dad before her accident? Had she been preparing us for what was happening with her?

"Hey, now," he pouted. Even his pout was sexy.

"I could be a dental hygienist," I thought out loud, sounding like José's mother. "Everyone has teeth!"

He laughed, sending a jolt of happiness through me. The carbonated cells were back.

"This was an emergency," he said. "I wanted to see you."

The sun was inside my stomach, bursting rays out from my intestines.

"And I needed a taco." He winked at me.

"A taco emergency," I concluded.

"It happens." We crunched on our tacos in Lula's. Our feet touching just enough to keep sending jolts of electricity straight to my heart.

I had it so bad for José. My feelings had evolved from a fantasy crush to actually having feelings for him as a real, live flawed human. And I wasn't sure if I loved or hated it.

CHAPTER TWENTY-THREE

I heard the front door clang shut and was glad I had put the Christmas bells on the door knob. My instincts had told me Nora would make a run for it one of these days and I wanted to at least hear her go. I never predicted it would be in the middle of the night, while dad was away at an insurance conference in Ohio. Thankfully, the bells rattled me awake.

I found her dancing around Fred's yard, waving colorful sarongs around, riling up the chickens and goats.

"Nora, it's late. We need to get some sleep," I hissed, wrapping my robe tighter around me, wishing I had put on shoes as the cold dirt stuck between my toes.

"I'm working," she said and continued to dance, shaking her hips and pulling her knees up like an aerobics instructor. Her mobility was impressive considering she couldn't bend much a month ago.

"It's a full moon and it's my job to encourage the animals to mate. Since I can't do my duties with the sea creatures, I'll work my persuasion on land."

Awesome. Maybe Nora could make a career of taking animals off the extinction list. She could eliminate endangered species by syncing with the lunar cycle. "Okay, is this going to take long? I've got a test tomorrow and really need my rest."

Keeping my voice calm, I tried to coax Nora back inside, but I couldn't compete with the full moon. Her employer.

"I'm going to make it rain. It's been really dry lately," she informed me while getting tangled in the scarves.

Rain? Like with a rain dance? Was Nora learning about Native American culture too?

"We conjure storms, you know. Its what mermaids do. We control the weather with our emotions," she continued while I helped unwrap the sarongs from her arms. My colorful mummy mom had yet another paranormal ability.

The last thing I wanted was to have the neighbors' witness my mother's rainmaking rituals. With my luck, Fred would wake up and join her, dancing under the light of the full moon. Naked.

Instead of witnessing a torrential downpour, I convinced Nora to come inside and counsel me on my relationship with José, and subsequently Savannah. Since I couldn't tell anybody else, I decided she was the safest confidant, and I figured mermaid counseling was the next best thing to maternal counseling. Nora assured me that mermaids were the best secret keepers, and so I proceeded to tell her every minute detail. It was elating to finally tell somebody that José and I had kissed, and Nora clapped and cheered for me almost as wildly as Kessia would have.

"But he's not really with Savannah?" she asked.

"No. It's just something is going on at home…with his mom. I'm not sure. So, he doesn't want to tell her they're broken up yet."

When I told her about ditching school to be with him, she didn't flinch because unlike attorneys, mermaids aren't concerned about perfect attendance and academia. But after about an hour, I wanted to go to bed.

Nora wanted to dance.

"I wouldn't dare sleep on such a night...I'm too lonely without my pirate. Where is he?" she asked, pouting.

"Toledo."

"Why isn't he here?" Her voice was whiney and her bottom lip shot out again."He's at a convention in Ohio...for pirates."

"I'm not sure he's really a pirate. He doesn't act like one at all."

No, he didn't. I really wished Dad would step it up around here. Or at least *be* here.

Nora finally climbed into bed once I promised to sleep with her. I put on the National Geographic channel so she could watch a sea life special. But just as I was drifting off, she started screaming.

"What is it, Mom? Are you in pain?!" I searched for blood as she wailed in agony.

"The turtles have herpes!"

I rewound the show a bit so that I could see and hear what she was upset about. There were turtles covered in disfiguring tumors, mostly on their heads and around their eyes.

"Oh no!" I gasped, learning that the STD infected turtles lived in a popular tourist destination off the coast of Australia. How was this possible?

"I have to get back," Nora was rocking again. "They need me."

I wasn't sure what a mermaid would do to save the pollution ridden waters, but I understood why Nora was deeply disturbed. The turtles were suffering with massive tumors covering their bodies. Humans had contaminated their environment, and the turtles were paying the ultimate price.

She pulled on my arms, squeezing tightly, "Promise me, you'll take me back!"

"Okay." I shook my arms free.

"I have to get back," she squeaked, collapsing into the bed.

Animal Planet had a show about puppies, so I switched to that, making sure nothing else would traumatize Nora. Or myself. I brought her a blanket and some tea, holding her hand until I passed out sometime before the sun came up.

DAD FACETIMED me five minutes before my alarm was set to go off and I was furious. I really needed those 300 seconds of REMs.

"How's it going, Pumpkin?" He looked freshly showered, his wet hair combed to the side, a new shirt on.

"Not good. I pulled the night shift with Mom." My tongue glided over my teeth like a scientist examining a new algae species that had appeared overnight. I tried to remember if I had brushed my teeth before bed. Or this week. My hygiene had taken a back seat since I'd become Nora's primary caregiver.

"Thanks, Em. I know it's not ideal." His teeth looked sparkly clean.

"Not ideal?" Was he on crack? I took the phone outside so Nora wouldn't hear me. My feet were those of a caveman, dirt outlining my toenails, from last night's full moon ritual.

"Dad, maybe we should put her in a treatment center. She really needs professional help and I can't do this by myself. She's not getting any better." I huffed while I talked, flapping my arms and catching a whiff of my own odor. It seemed my Nora care-taking and the stress was causing my sweat glands to work over-time and the resulting smell was pretty badly.

"Em, you're being overly dramatic. I'll be home in a few days and give you a break." He ran a clean, dry hand through his wet hair and grinned. I bet he probably had good dreams and a free continental breakfast.

I went back inside while I yelled, no longer carrying if Nora heard me, stomping through the house.

"I'm being overly dramatic?!?! You brought her home and you're never here! She doesn't believe you are a pirate at all. No, my mother thinks she controls the climate and the weather and animal mating rituals and I'm being overly dramatic. Really?!?! Did you get a good night sleep, Dad? Do you have a science test you couldn't study for because you were up all night learning about full moon mermaid obligations?"

"Em. Emily, wait..." He called out from the hotel room in Toledo.

"No, I have to get ready for school." I looked at him one last time before I passed the phone to Mom, who was just waking up.

"Nora, it's Bart." My voice sounded like a million snakes were speaking for me as I hissed, "He wants to hear *all* about the turtle herpes."

Slamming the bathroom door and cranking on the hot water helped release my rage, but I couldn't escape my life. My situation was not going to disappear while I washed the dirt down the drain. And I could hear Nora wailing from underneath the shower water.

CHAPTER TWENTY-FOUR

The shower hadn't washed away my wall of anxiety and there wasn't enough coffee in the world to wake me enough to take my test and get a decent grade. I internally debated skipping school, which gave me even more anxiety. It was layers and layers of stress stacking up inside my body.

I shoved cereal into my mouth while I went through the piles of mail on the table, sorting them into what looked like important things Dad needed to deal with and junk mail. The DNA kit had arrived and I had missed it. I tore open the box and skimmed the direction, learning Nora needed to spit in to a tube before she ate anything.

Running into her bedroom, DNA kit in hand, I found Nora the Mermaid and Amy deep into something on her laptop. They slammed it shut as I entered. A sure sign of guilt.

"What's going on?" I asked, feeling odd that I was in the parental role and my mother was not. I reached for the laptop and Amy pulled it away, convincing me more than ever, I had to see what they were up to.

Ripping the laptop from Amy's grip, perhaps a bit too aggressively, I put the DNA kit on the nightstand while I opened the computer and examined the pages that were open on the screen.

"We were just looking," Amy lied.

Apparently BIGDADDY42JK97 had a truck and would drive Nora and Amy to the Pacific Ocean. He could pick them up as soon as he had the address and a magic card number.

"Oh my God! You two were going to hitch a ride with a stranger off the internet!" I screamed at a level I'd never reached before. "Are you absolutely crazy? You could be killed! Murdered. Oh my God, I can't even." I felt bile rising in my throat. A deep fear rose up my neck.

"Big Daddy 42 something seemed really nice," Nora explained. "He was only going to charge us for gas."

"Nora, you were being catfished."

"I get along great with catfish." She looked to Amy. "You'd really like them. I don't know why they have a bad reputation. They're nice. You'll see."

"You will not see!" I clicked on report to flag BigDaddy as a scammer online and searched their correspondence for how much information they had given whoever they were. Fortunately, no addresses or credit card numbers had been shared. Catastrophe adverted, for now, but I still couldn't calm down. How was I going to keep Nora safe and in Nebraska?

"Amy, finish getting ready for school." For once she didn't argue with me and scurried out of the bedroom.

Opening the DNA test, I walked to where Nora was seated on the bed. "I need you to spit in this vial to the red line."

"I can't," Nora pulled the sheets up around her mouth.

"It's for my science class. I'm going to fail if you don't do this!" I made up out of nowhere.

"I can't let you clone me," she declared as if we were living in a sci-fi movie.

What?!? Nora thought I wanted to clone her? "What are you talking about? Why would I want to clone you?" I smoothed down my hair, trying to be calming although I was a bunch of boiling cells, "I promise you, Nora. Cloning you is the last thing I would want to do. Honest."

"I saw a show about cloning sheep. I know how popular mermaids are and I just can't do that to another mermaid. I can't condemn them to a life away from the sea. Nebraska is beautiful, but I want to go home. I need to be home." She was crying, her entire frame shaking.

Wrapping my arms around to comfort her, I held my mother's shrinking frame. "It's gonna be okay," I said, wanting to believe the words myself. "I won't force another mermaid to live away from the sea."

"You'll take me to the Pacific Ocean?" She looked hopeful through her wet eyes.

"Yes." I made the promise, but it was an empty one. I had no intention whatsoever of taking Nora to the Pacific Ocean, or any ocean for that matter. She was my mother and all I wanted was to reset her memory. "As long as you promise not to talk to ANYONE on the internet ever again, I'll take you."

"Then I'll spit in the tube."

"You will!?!" Digging the tube back out of the kit, I handed it to her, praying she wouldn't change her mind until I collected all the evidence required.

Once Nora spit to the red line of the tube, I added the necessary solution provided and closed the tube. Following the instructions, I placed the tube into the return box and sealed it safely shut. I'd add the post office to our route today and drop the box into the drive-through mail box. In two to four weeks, I'd be closer to having my mother back.

"It's after nine," Amy announced in the doorway, so proud of herself for learning to tell time. "We are late."

We were late. And I wasn't about to leave Nora alone after she'd almost given our address to a stranger online. I checked my phone and Kessia had gotten a ride to school with Stud Muffin Jack. There really wasn't a reason I had to go to school other than that test I'd most likely fail, but Nora was going to have to call in my absence. I was too angry at Dad to ask him to do it. He had no idea that we could have lost Amy and Nora to an online predator. It made me rage to even think about.

"You girls are staying home today?!" Nora clapped her hands together. "We're going to have so much fun!"

Her emotional roller coaster was making me even more exhausted. Amy looked at me, waiting expectantly to see if she was ditching too. I nodded yes, "We're staying home."

I dialed my school attendance number and decided to talk Nora through the process while it rang. "Since technically you're my biological mother, I need you to tell the school I'm sick so I won't get in trouble."

"Are you sick?" Nora asked concerned.

"No. Well, sort of. Just say it, please. Okay, she's answering." I hit speakerphone.

"Hello, Mayview High School, this is Marian. With whom am I speaking with?"

"Nora the Mermaid."

"Um, okay. How can I help you?"

"Emily is sick. Sort of. She won't be at school today and I don't want her to be in trouble."

"Oh. All right then. Thank you for calling, Nora the Mermaid. I hope you have a nice day."

Nora pressed the red button and hung up the phone. "See, I did it! Did I do a good job pretending to be your mother?"

"Yes. Thank you, Nora." I said, even though her words pricked at my open emotional wound. My mother was proud of herself for pretending to be my mother. So what that out of about a thousand other Emilys at my school the attendance lady knew it was my mother that had morphed into a mermaid. At least I wasn't truant I kept telling myself. Ya gotta find that silver lining somewhere.

CHAPTER TWENTY-FIVE

After a day of witnessing Nora and Fred paint the living room wall with clear paint and glitter and then hot-glue seashells all over the coffee table, it was time to take Amy to her dance class. I insisted Nora join us since I wasn't ready to let her out of my sight, so Fred tagged along, climbing into my passenger seat.

"I just don't know why you have to be so angry all the time," Nora said as Amy helped her buckle her seatbelt.

Was I angry? Or was I just stressed out. It's not like I know how to wrangle a landlocked mermaid on top of everything else I need to get done.

It was like walking on eggshells around her. The slightest argument could break this once fiery attorney who used to eat abusive parents for breakfast. Her frailty scared me. I grew up believing Nora was invincible. This warrior who could take on anything and now she was afraid of her own shadow.

"Do mermaids have blubber?" Amy asked, rubbing Nora's hand and soothing her. "Or do they migrate like whales?"

Back in her comfort zone, Nora sat up straight. "Yes, kind of like penguins. Mermaids have high body temperatures too and keep active." She looked at Amy with adoring eyes, like her mother. Amy had always been the baby of the family, but seeing her connect with Nora the Mermaid stung my heart.

"Do mermaids sleep swim?" Amy dug deeper. She seemed to have no memory of our mother raising us and had thrown herself fully into this make-believe fantasy that Nora just showed up a few weeks ago from the ocean. I'd have to keep a close eye on Amy. If she was this gullible she may be susceptible to joining a cult. "How do you swim while you sleep? Do you bump into things?"

My eyes rolled so far back into my head it hurt. A part of me wished Amy would stop connecting to the mermaid part of mom, as if she was encouraging the behavior, even though I knew Amy had no control of it.

"Babs loved this car," Fred said to me and I was glad to not have to focus on the mermaid banter any longer. "She'd like that you have it now, Emily. She always liked you."

"Thanks, Fred." It was weird to think of Babs now that she had passed. She was always nice to me and Amy, but it was mom that took care of her when she got really sick.

"She sure loved your mom." He chuckled to himself. "…But she would have really adored Nora the Mermaid. Wish she was here now."

"I'm sorry, Fred." And I was. It must be hard to lose your wife and best friend at the same time. "Do you think she's in a better place?"

Fred took a deep breath and exhaled before he answered, "Better than Nebraska? Oh, that's hard to imagine, but I'd like to think so."

I could think of about a million places better than Nebraska. Probably almost any place on Earth, but I couldn't confirm that as I hadn't traveled out of the state lines.

"She's with us. I can feel her spirit," Fred said, and then turned his gaze out the window.

I really liked Babs when she was alive and all, and I get that this was her car, but it made me queasy to think that a ghost was my co-pilot.

"Emily is going to take me," Nora announced, breaking me from my vision of the exorcism I'd have to do in my car. "She promised."

"I did. That's right." I forced a smile. "I'll be taking Nora to the Pacific Ocean soon, Fred. I just need your help keeping her safe until that day."

"You can't go yet!" Amy exclaimed as we pulled into her dance studio parking lot. "You'll miss my recital!"

I found myself praying for the millionth time today, please let Nora stay for the recital. Anything to keep her motivated to stay in Nebraska till I got the DNA test results back and worked on my case.

"Oh, what's a recital?" Nora asked as she got out of the car.

We quickly learned all about the recital from Amy's very annoyed dance teacher who was trying to pacify twelve little girls who wanted to be princesses since they had a "special guest mermaid queen." Nora caused quite the commotion with her mermaid crown, so the dance teacher passed out prop tiaras for the girls to wear for this "special occasion."

"Can the mermaid dance with us?" One little girl asked and the rest squealed with excitement.

"Just for today," the dance teacher said through gritted teeth, a painfully forced smile. "Just for today, right?!" She looked in my direction. "She's a bit of a…distraction."

"Agreed." I nodded as I spoke, feeling sorry for her unplanned day of chaos.

Nora seemed to cause a maelstrom wherever she went and was completely oblivious to those of us left to clean up the aftermath. She danced along with the girls and spun a few of them around. When their parents came to pick them up, Nora lined up and hugged each little princess good-bye.

After class, the dance teacher reiterated that Nora could not dress as a mermaid for the Mother's Day recital. They were implementing a strict "no mermaid" policy effective immediately, but wanted to make sure that I understood they were not discriminating. In fact, they were making it "no dress-up" for anyone other than students – period.

As one little girl left the class she cried to her mother, "I want a mermaid crown!"

Her mother gently pulled her towards the parking lot, "Me too, Sweetie. Me too."

"You can get them online!" Nora shouted. "It's magical!"

She hugged Amy again, "That was the best dance class ever. I want to come to every single one!"

Amy looked at the dance teacher with wide eyes, but I interjected. "We'll find you a different class, Nora. One for mermaids." I gathered Fred, Nora and Amy and headed out of the dance studio, pretty sure that the dance teacher would be hitting the cocktails tonight.

We returned Fred home to the chickens and goat and planted Nora in front of the TV. *Tanked* reruns were on and they were making an enormous fish tank out of a treasure chest for an actor. Amy was helping me make dinner. I was proud that it was entirely vegan, and tasted amazing so far.

I was feeling pretty good about keeping it all together. Both Nora and Amy seemed happy and my anxiety was taking the night off. I was rocking this family crisis.

But Bart came in and stole my thunder.

He was dressed as a pirate, carrying a big, gold sword, and actually looked quite dashing in his white, loose flowing shirt. Seeing Dad's chest hair was jolting and he had a fake earring dangling from one ear. At least, I was assuming it was fake. His striped pants were tucked into buckled, worn boots, and he was pulling off this *Pirates of the Caribbean* look a little bit too well.

Nora was obviously taken with Bart the Pirate's good looks

and the two of them retreated into their bedroom. It was like those provocative movies they played late at night on cable, and being that it was my parents, it was totally and completely revolting. Nora and Bart may have been headed for a divorce, but the mermaid and pirate seemed to be doing just fine.

CHAPTER TWENTY-SIX

The annual Lake McConaughy Fishing Tournament was happening this year without Dad competing. He was supposed to check-in before the crack of dawn, but Nora had a meltdown about him using live bait.

"Worms and frogs have feelings too," she cried. "Especially frogs. They're really sensitive."

Dad was a good sport about it and withdrew from the competition. He loved his fishing tournaments and had been an avid fisherman his entire life. I remember that he used to take Amy and I along with him on early morning outings. I'd put neon, smelly bait on my toes and watch the fish nibble as I'd dangled my feet in the water. But now, he had to tend to his mermaid wife and keep her from escaping to the Pacific Ocean. It was Dad's turn to step it up around here.

"Too bad she doesn't think she's a bass; You could have won the tournament."

"Emily!" Dad said, but then kind of chuckled. I can only assume he was thinking of Nora the same way I was, as an enormous bass with a hook in her mouth. "We're leaving in ten, Matey." Now, he was taking his pirate role far too seriously.

"Okay, bye." I added a wave for good measure.

"Emily, you're coming. Family outing."

"Oh, now we're a family...that does family things. Okay."

My dad wasn't the least bit embarrassed about my mom's altered reality. She was parading around town dressed as a mermaid and he didn't even flinch. I was starting to think he liked it, like in a weird way. How could he possibly like the different colored mermaid scale leggings she wore every day and the shell bra t-shirts? She even decorated her flip-flops with shells and starfish. And the crowns really got me. A massive crown on her head like she was some kind of underwater royalty. They're just so obnoxious.

Old Nora would be embarrassed of her new self. I was mortified. Each time I had to be seen with her was torturous. My stomach hurt and my ears burned with shame.

"We are going in public?!? Again?" I hadn't even recovered from the dance studio yet. Why would we keep doing that to ourselves? When was this constant humiliation going to end?

"Yes, Emily, and I'd dress as King Titan if it made your mother happy."

So Dad had gone from a missing person to being her guardian. I guess I should be relieved that he was taking the weight off my shoulders, but it kind of annoyed me. No thanks for all the work I'd put in thus far keeping Nora from harming herself, or Amy.

The mermaid herself walked in, witnessing Dad's newfound, everlasting devotion to her emotional status.

"You're not wearing your pirate clothes?"

Ten minutes later, we loaded into the car; Amy and I, and our parents, Bart the Pirate and Nora the Mermaid.

Amy giggled at the absurdity of our situation, which I assumed was nerves. Who were we going to run into? How could we act like we didn't know them? Would we ever rid ourselves of the stigma of our wackadoodle parents?

I know most teenagers find their parents embarrassing, but

if there was a contest, I'd win. This takes the cake. I'd managed to remain invisible through most my life, but now I was thrust into the spotlight. It was like we were living in a parade, my parents being the grandest, most obnoxiously decorated float, and my sister and I were being dragged along for the ride.

Dad pulled into the Pawnee Plunge parking lot and Amy and I exchanged fearful glances. We were definitely going to run into people we knew. This was the most popular water park in Columbus, and basically *the* place to hang out and cool off.

Everyone stared as we made our way to some empty lounge chairs. I could feel the pity from strangers, and the judgment.

A woman wearing a big, floppy hat and gynormous glasses flagged us down.

"Nora, you look wonderful!" she squawked. "We miss you at work."

Nora nodded politely, "Hello."

"Thanks, Gale," Dad responded, directing Nora in the opposite direction. "Hopefully, she'll be back soon."

"Do I know her?" Nora whispered.

"Yes, Sweetheart."

"I don't remember."

"It's okay." Dad rubbed Nora's shoulders. "Let's have some fun!"

"Great," I thought. Now Mom's other co-workers were going to keep looking at us like one of their charity cases. "We don't need any more casseroles," I wanted to scream, but in reality, we did need them because Nora was no longer allowed inside our local grocery store.

Maybe Gale should be added to my expert witness list. She knew mom as an attorney at Child Protective Services. I made a mental note to contact her down the road if needed for my case.

Bart and Nora dashed off like teenagers, racing to the lines of the biggest slide. They were going to have the time of their lives today, frolicking in the water, like absolutely nothing was wrong. They didn't care about Amy and I at all!

Some of the kids were delighted when Bart joined them on the Pirate Ship, running and screaming in mock fear. He pretended to kidnap Nora, carrying her to the top of the ship while the kids cheered.

Amy and I watched them in silence for awhile, until she abandoned me to join them in the splash pool. Apparently, her eternal embarrassment didn't run as deep as mine.

Traitor.

I covered my head with a towel and lost myself in way-too-loud music. At least I could escape from my obnoxious parents in my mind. I hadn't seen anyone from school yet, and figured if I kept my head covered, no one would ever know I was here.

CHAPTER TWENTY-SEVEN

"You're getting burnt," Dad spooked me by yanking one of my earphones from my ear. Ouch. I flipped over to talk to him, noticing he'd lost buttons from his pirate shirt. And thankfully, the gold hoop earring was gone, but the soggy eye patch survived.

"Aren't you going to try the double loop tube slide?"

"Maybe later," I answered. We both watched as Amy and Nora came barreling out of a slide together. "Why did we wait for mom to be a mermaid to have some family fun?"

"Good question. Sometimes we need a good kick in the Pirate's Booty. A wake-up call, I guess."

I ignored his geeky joke and focused on the wake-up call segment. A wake-up call for what? Was mom's life so bad before her accident? What was dad waking up from?

"You're a good kid, Emily. Your mom would be proud."

"What about Nora the Mermaid?"

"I don't know, Love. I have no idea what's going on in that head."

"I'm worried she's going to leave." My voice cracked and I felt a huge lump in my throat.

"She promised she'd stay till Amy's recital. We've bought some more time for the doctors to keep working with her. And I don't know, Em. We have to just keep moving forward."

I knew he was right on some level, but I couldn't shake the fear that my mom was a flight risk. It was only a matter of time before she figured out how to get a train ticket. Or an Uber. Thankfully my dad was back and on top of it. And Fred had promised to be my eyes and ears. At least eyes and ears working at about a fifty percent capacity, but it was something.

Dad pulled me up and guided me reluctantly to the largest slide at the park. I begrudgingly allowed it to happen, but I refused to have fun on principle.

The slide was a lot faster and more powerful than I expected. I choked on water as I was tossed into the pool, yanking my bottoms up since the water was forcing them down. Only, I didn't have enough hands to keep my bikini top secure as well. Unlike my mother, I didn't have sea creature capabilities like that of an octopus.

I crouched down in the water, trying to adjust my triangles to cover the proper body parts, when a kid plowed into me and knocked me over. Awesome, I thought as I swallowed gallons of disgusting public pool water.

"Emily!" I heard as I took a breath and immediately dove back underwater, slowly coming up like a periscope behind an inner tube.

I scanned the perimeter and quickly spotted José and his family by a table with balloons and streamers. I ducked down like a submarine, moving from the safety of one jellyfish float to another.

Pulling myself out of the water, I tried to creep back to my towel to hide, but the pavement was too hot and I threw myself as ungracefully as possible back into the water.

"Hey, Emily," José called out from the outskirts of the pool. He looked all gorgeous and sun-kissed, his skin a deep, dark brown. His shorts hung dangerously low, revealing those impressive lower ab muscles just above the hips that form a solid V. I swooned.

"Hey."

"It's my nephew's birthday. Come have some cake?"

I could do that. He offered a hand as I climbed out of the water and I felt a slight thrill as this was the first time we'd been together in our swimsuits.

"Hey, Emily." The voice was saccharin sweet and could only belong to Savannah. Here I was a wet dog and she hadn't gotten a drop of water on her perfectly coiffed hair. "It's chocolate cake. I made it last night."

Of course she did. She was perfect. Add baking to the long list of skills she already possessed. And she was an integral part of José's family. Of course she would be there.

José's nephew popped over, "You're Emily, right?"

I nodded, "Happy Birthday."

"So, your mom really thinks she's a mermaid?"

I nodded again. "Yeah, it's kind of strange. Right?"

"You're turning pink," Savannah said. "Want to use some of my sunscreen?"

I looked sunburned, but really it was the color of humiliation. Crimson red. My blood rushed to my face and chest, making me splotchy. Sunscreen couldn't save my ears as they burned from the inside out.

This must be what the person who had the diarrhea accident at the water park last summer experienced. They had to close the place down for three days while they sanitized. Why didn't anyone take a big poop in the floating river right now so I could slip away?

Savannah smiled sweetly at me. It must be what the person who is flicking the switch to the electric chair does right before they turn it on. "We really should hang out, Em. Like, really, really."

She was going to kill me. In public. It was official and

couldn't be more real. She'd have alibis, as everyone loved her. I was so toast.

Tasha, Savannah's mom, and Amelia, José's mom joined us. They each wore a designer swimsuit with a sarong tied around their waists. Since they'd been best friends for over forty years, they could finish each other's sentences, and since they were co-presidents of the PTA for the past decade, they knew each kids' personal business.

"Emily, how are you? How's your mom?" Tashsa asked.

"Good. She's okay," I answered automatically, seeking out my mother and finding her perched on a rock.

Couldn't they see her spouting the dirtiest-water-on-the-planet out of her mouth like a fountain? She'd probably get Typhoid Fever and die tonight, but at least we'd all be out of our misery. Please God don't strike me down for thinking this. It's not like I want it to happen. Not really.

It's just that I've never been more uncomfortable with Savannah, José, and their moms all staring at me. Savannah, smiling like an angel, pretending we're friends after she filmed my mother's mermaid illness on Snapchat. Only an evil witch would do that, in my opinion. All I knew was that I had to get away from her.

Where was my escape? Why hadn't a teenager dumped an entire bottle of dish soap into the floating river? How awesome would a bubble explosion be, creating the perfect distraction so that I could run away unnoticed? Where were the rebels when you needed one?

"I think it's so touching that your dad is dressing like a pirate," Tasha said, her hand over her heart to stress she had all the feels.

"Thanks." It wasn't touching; it was weird. Maybe if I held my breath I'd pass out.

"Amelia, what is it?" Tasha looked to her best friend, concerned.

"I don't think Manuel loves me like that," Amelia sobbed.

"You're his heart," Tasha comforted.

"He would never put on a pirate costume and run around a water park." Big tears fell from her eyes, not even smudging her waterproof mascara. "I don't think we're going to make it. He's…he's…said the D word more than once."

All eyes went to Amelia and I made my exit quickly, mumbling something about having to go somewhere. With burning feet, I raced to my towel and then continued all the way to the car. I waited there, sweltering in the backseat until the rest of my oddball family finally made their way out of Pawnee Plunge.

CHAPTER TWENTY-EIGHT

I was able to get Nora into Dr. Sy's waiting room at a faster
pace by bribing her with Janet's tapioca, holding the spoon
just out in front of her like a fish hook. "Come on, Nora," I
coaxed, luring her in.

"Emily, why don't you join our session today?"

"No thanks, I've got mermaid overload." Is that a thing? I
looked on WebMD, but didn't find it. That or mermaid
aversion.

"Come in," she commanded, and I did. Maybe it would
help wake up my mom. Dr. Sy could be an integral part of my
case as she has Nora's trust. Mom's always said you can't have
too many expert witnesses on your side.

Nora and I squished onto a loveseat, pillows surrounding us.
Dr. Sy offered one of us to move to a chair, or us both to the
bigger couch, but we remained crammed uncomfortably
together.

"What if she thought she was a snail? Or a dog? Would that
be better?" she asked.

"No. If she thought she was my mother. That would be
better," I answered.

"Maybe the question you could ask yourself is, 'Why does she want to be a mermaid?'" Dr. Sy leaned towards us as she spoke.

"Okay."

"Mermaids symbolize unconscious depths and all things feminine, such as sensuality, love, magic, beauty...the extraordinary." She studied me, waiting for a reaction, so I purposely pokerfaced it. "They remind us about the pitfalls of temptations...and, they show us humans how challenging it is to bring our unconscious worlds into our realities."

"Huh?" I tried not to blink.

"In shrink speak, what I mean is that your mom has buried information in her subconscious that is too painful to deal with so her brain is protecting her. Hence, the mermaid persona."

"Okay," I repeated.

"Emily, your mom is a challenging case. I'm not sure what exactly is going on and we're nowhere near a diagnosis of any sort."

"Can't you give her a pill or something?"

"There are no magic pills. Medications work when there's a specific problem to address, say anxiety or depression."

"Okay. I just want my mother back. No offense to Nora the Mermaid."

Nora smiled at me warmly, and then looked back to Dr. Sy.

"Why? You're practically a woman yourself. In some cultures a 16-year-old would be married and having children."

"Gross. I thought I had a few more years to be a teenager. Just hang out and be carefree."

"So, you're mad at Nora because you feel you're being robbed of your teenage years?"

"Yeah, I guess." Was she putting words in my mouth? Was that what I really thought? I wasn't sure.

"How else do you feel?" Dr. Sy pressed, hitting all my emotional triggers by the arrogance I interpreted in her voice.

"About what?" I knew what she was asking, but I didn't want to answer. I couldn't access all my thoughts and feelings swirling inside me and make a coherent sentence.

"Mermaids."

"Don't they trick men? Seems odd that Nora, who always preached feminism, would pick a kind of trampy creature to become. It's kind of out of character." I challenged Dr. Sy, grateful that this thought had dominated through my clustered mind. Weren't mermaids promiscuous, shamefully vain, and dare I even think it…slutty?

"Mermaids are known to be honest. And discerning. Can't a woman be both attractive and honorable?" She tossed her thought back at me.

"Yes, a woman can be beautiful and smart…and honest… and everything. But we are talking about mermaids. This mermaid," I pointed to Nora in case anyone was confused about who the mermaid in the room was. "She doesn't remember that she is my mother. I miss her."

"Nora, how does this make you feel? Does my conversation with Emily evoke any memories? Or thoughts?" Dr. Sy asked Nora, her voice definitely kinder toward my mom, whom she obviously liked better than me.

"I want her to be happy." Nora sighed.

"Then stop acting like a fish," I said. Duh, it's that simple. For some reason, I couldn't talk about how scared I was that Nora was never going to remember me. It hurt too much to even say the words. "Are we done, Dr. Sy?"

"I want to go home, too. My real home," Nora whined, as if Dr. Sy would take her there if she asked enough times.

She was wringing her hands and gazing out the window. I knew she was hoping that she could see the Pacific Ocean in the distance, which was impossible. I didn't need a shrink to tell me that even mermaids get depressed.

CHAPTER TWENTY-NINE

"Do you really want to work on our project today?" José asked as he exited his house, moving towards me so fast my heart started beating double time.

I shook my head no, leaning against my car I had just parked in front of his house. I honestly didn't, but I wanted to spend time with José.

"Let's go."

He grabbed my hand and pulled me to his truck. Kissing me before opening my door and holding it open for me.

It was the most thrilling few moments of my life. His touch alone was able to erase all other memories and replace them with this one moment, as insignificant as it may appear to an observer. But it was my moment.

We drove through town and out to the lake, watching the sun tuck in and out of the clouds, stopping at Barneys Tackle & Bait to get worms and sub sandwiches.

"I like a girl who can fish," he said, both hands on the steering wheel and eyes on the gravel road. I beamed, grateful for all of Dad's lessons.

Parking by the jetty, we unloaded the fishing gear and José

neatly placed a blanket down for us to sit on. He watched as I looped my worm onto my hook like a pro.

"RIP, Wormy," I said.

José made the Catholic cross with his right hand, "In the name of the Father and of the Son and of the Holy Spirit. Amen."

"Thank you," I said, unable to remove the grin from my face.

"For what?" He asked.

"Respecting my worm's eminent death," I said. Maybe it was dumb, but I always said a little thank you prayer for the worm whose life I was sacrificing to catch a fish.

"Life is life."

Was it weird that I fell for him even harder because he cared about something so small and helpless? It made my head float as if I'd sucked the air out of a helium balloon.

I cast my hook as far as I was able, enjoying the plop sounds as it sank into the water, and loving that we had this section of the lake all to ourselves. Just us and the bugs.

Swat. I killed a mosquito on my cheek.

"I'm gonna catch the biggest fish," I predicted out loud, feeling cocky.

"Is that so?" he scoffed, bumping me with his body.

"I feel lucky," I said, wanting more contact. I scooted closer to him so that our sides were touching, his breath slowed and synchronized with mine.

"Me too," he said as he cast his line. "Real lucky."

He was looking at me, but I wasn't entirely sure if he was talking about me or the fish.

"How's the career search going?"

"Good. I'm considering hazardous waste removal." I'd read about disgusting jobs that pay well before bed last night. It was still fresh in my mind, and easy to recall.

"Yeah, you're into that?" he asked, clearly not convinced.

"If I invest in a suit, I can do both hazardous waste removal and crime scene clean up." Honestly, if I could handle any sort of blood it wouldn't be a bad career option. The news showed people dying all the time and someone had to clean it up, however morbid that may be.

He just laughed, and then swatted another mosquito away.

"Hey, it gives me lots of options. I'd never be bored. I'd meet interesting people. Imagine the flexible hours. And I could make multiple business cards." Was I building a case for my fake waste removal business as if I were Nora? Was it second nature for me to justify every piece of nonsense out of my mouth? I couldn't wait for those DNA tests to return. Stat.

"There'd be blood, Emily," he said gently, tucking flying away hairs behind my ear, simultaneously setting it on fire. It kept tingling even after he removed his hand.

"And goo. And whatever else qualifies as toxic waste," I responded, mentally begging the wind to set those flyaways free so he could tuck them back again.

"I think you should keep looking." But he was focused on his fishing pole, reeling it in two cranks.

"Expand my search?" I checked my own pole, but it didn't need any adjustments. I wondered if the worm was still wrapped around the hook. My José blessed worm.

"Yeah. Like a lot." He turned his attention back to me.

I liked how he looked at me. I liked our banter, and how I didn't have to be serious all the time.

We sat in silence, being still, like true Zen fishermen. There was a peacefulness in watching the ripples and listening to the evening bugs sing and buzz.

My pole started to dance and shake. I gripped it with my left hand and cranked the line with my right, using my feet to hold the bottom of my pole in place. It slipped from my knees' grip.

"You got it," José cheered.

I stayed focus, reeling steadily.

"Here," José wrapped his arms around me and helped me hold my ground with the massive fish.

Plunk.

We both fell backwards, me on top of him, as my line snapped. I struggled to roll off him, hitting his face with my pole.

"Oh, I'm so sorry." I stayed on top of him, "José?"

He held his nose. I saw blood trickle down.

"José, you're bleeding," I dug my knees onto the ground between us and began to lift myself off him.

"I'm okay," he wiped his face with his sleeve and pulled me back on top of him and kissed me.

We kissed for minutes, savoring each other's lips and body heat and breath. His kisses were the only drug that took me away from my reality, from all the chaos in my family, and the suffering when I wasn't locked in his embrace.

Even though I'd lost the fish, and the worm had surely met his maker, I still felt really, really lucky.

CHAPTER THIRTY

M r. Edward's sub looked legit lost as she backed into the classroom holding a campus map. Her crow's feet, dated hairstyle, and comfort shoes clashed with the gazillion stacking rings on her fingers. Placing her computer bag on Mr. Edward's desk, she picked up his lesson plan and then assessed the room.

"This is English, right? Okay. How did we go from Shakespeare to incomprehensible texting?"

Was she expecting an answer from a group of bored teenagers?

"Using emojis instead of words…does anyone actually speak English anymore?" she continued, as if anyone cared.

Mr. Edward's was absent, so it was basically a free hour to relax or do homework, depending on which side of the universe you fell into.

We split into groups, chatting as if the substitute didn't exist. Kessia scooted her desk next to mine and whipped out her phone, showing me her latest test from Jack, who was two rows behind us.

"Shhhh. Don't let him see you reading."

If he had eyes, he could see me reading, but I wasn't going to state the obvious.

The substitute attached her phone to the smart board with a USB cord. A screenshot of a text from someone named Roger appeared on the screen.

Right, babe, it read, punctuated by a laughing tears emoji.

"Hello, I'm a teacher. I'm in charge here." She grabbed Mr. Edward's pool stick by his desk, and banged it on a student's desk.

"Okay. Hello. Thank you for your attention." She pointed the pool stick toward the screen displaying the test. "Now, is Pacman crying? I need some translation here, please."

"That's laughing emoji," Kessia responded. "Like, laughing so hard you cry."

"That's laughing? I thought it was crying. But they're happy tears? How can you tell them apart from sad tears?" She studied the emoji up close. "They should make one that pees. You know...laughing so hard you pee."

"Gross," someone said from the back of class.

"Just wait till you have babies, ladies. You'll see what I mean."

And she clicked the remote, moving on to her next screenshot. This time a text from a person named Adam appeared. While she moved to the opposite side of the classroom to find out what the other emojis meant, Kessia took back her phone.

"Savannah would use that emoji. The peeing one."

"Stop," I regretted telling her the pee story for the millionth time. "She was six."

"Seriously. Savannah could wear a diaper and the next day half the school would be wearing them."

"Didn't you ever wet the bed?"

"She'd make Depends lit. And you know that's the truth."

Savannah did have that type of popularity power. I wanted to ask Kessia if she thought I should meet her for a coffee, but I couldn't. I was having a hard enough time not making googley eyes at José. Just hearing his voice as he spoke with Jack made my insides swirl.

"Hey. Rainbow braids. How do I know if he likes me?" The sub zeroed in on Kessia.

"Who?" Kessia asked.

"Roger, my first date since my divorce. Pay attention." The sub teacher hit the pool stick on Kessia's desk. I instinctively backed away, not wanting her to poke my eye out or something.

"When he introduces you to his friends, you're in," Kessia said.

"Oh. What if he wants to keep our relationship 'private'? Just between us?" She leaned in close, holding her breath before Kessia responded.

"If you're a secret, he's seeing other people too…or he has a girlfriend."

"Oh. Or he's married." She sighed. Disgust on her face.

"Right, old people problems," Kessia whispered to me.

"Damn those emoji Pacmans." The sub said and left the room while texting. She just walked out as if her job was done.

"Class is dismissed," Jack announced, getting up and leaving, stopping to wink at Kessia. Many others followed suit, filing out of class.

"Let's go," Kessia said, pulling on her backpack. "What a freak of a sub."

"Yeah," I agreed, shuffling out into the hallway.

"Who doesn't know when a guy really likes you or not?" Kessia scoffed. "Loser."

I didn't.

My situation with José was…complicated. I exhaled my frustration, and tried to hold onto what José and I were building. He wasn't with Savannah; he had promised another hundred times when we were fishing. And so far, I had no reason not to believe him…but did I really believe him? Why do I feel so amazing when I'm with him, and so terrible when I'm not?

CHAPTER THIRTY-ONE

A two-toned 1984 Ford-150 was parked in front of Fred's. At first I thought maybe a vet was visiting, but my instincts told me something was very off. The truck had dents around the back fender and a rusted grill on the front, so probably not a vet's. I dropped my backpack on the curb and hurried over, petting a goat as I ran to Fred's porch.

"Nora, where is your car?"

"I traded it." A bunch of furry animals slept in a make-shift pouch in her lap. Were they guinea pigs? Chinchillas? Had Nora gotten ferrets?

"She got just what she wanted for transporting the animals." Fred swept the porch in slow motion. Everything Fred did was in slow-mo.

"We met him at a fruit stand," Nora continued. "And he gave me a bunny."

"Oh, Mom. This is bad. That's not a good deal."

"I only paid for three rabbits and got four. That's a great deal. And they came in a crate so we already set them up in the backyard. I'll put them away after their nap."

She wasn't as enthusiastic as she'd been in the past, and seemed tired.

"The car. What about your car?"

"I traded it for the truck. Aren't you listening to me, Emily?"

"Show me the paperwork. The titles. I'll call dad or the police or something."

"Why, Emily?"

"You got bamboozled."

"I did?" She perked up, sitting straighter on the bench, shifting the sleeping bunnies. "That sounds amazing. I love that."

"It's not a good thing." My head throbbed. My eyes stung. The air in my lungs felt heavy. It was like my entire body was going on strike, one section at a time.

"It sounds spectacular. Right, Fred? We got bamboozled. I want to do it again."

"Bamboozled," Fred said, letting it roll off his tongue.

"Bamboozled," Nora said again, and I pretty much blew a fuse..

I stormed towards our house, grabbing my backpack and flinging it at the door. I couldn't do this anymore. I couldn't keep her out of trouble. No one was keeping her under control. She was my mother, and she was supposed to take care of me.

"I give up!" I yelled at the sky.

Dad pulled up, home from work, with Amy in tow. They took their time getting out of the car, gathering Amy's dance attire and school supplies that scattered about.

"Look at this! She traded her Lexus for this piece-of-junk." Pointing at the truck with both hands. "She's a beaut, all right."

Dad ran his hands through his hair, flustered. "I can't stop working and watch her all day, Emily. What do you want me to do?"

"Take away her credit cards for starters!" Duh. When did dad stop thinking rationally?

"She didn't charge the truck."

"I don't know. Just do something!"

"What? Your mother thinks she's a mermaid, Em. We're taking her to doctors. I'm dressing as a pirate. I'm trying here. I'm doing my best." He dropped all of Amy's tutus onto the driveway and bent to pick them up.

"I'm just so tired of it! I want her to stop." I wrapped my arms over my eyes as if that would make everything go away.

Amy went past us towards Fred's. "Fighting about it isn't helping."

"There are bunnies," I called to her. Amy loved rabbits and would be overjoyed. As an April born baby, Easter has always been her favorite holiday.

"At least the animals are keeping her here." Dad kicked the curb with one foot. "She wants to leave, you know."

"Yeah, she's promised to stay till Amy's recital. Mother's Day. Such a joke." I tried not to cry. I didn't want to cry all the time.

"I've been begging Fred not to take her. I'm afraid he's gonna cave. He's so lonely with Babs gone, I think if Nora asks him enough...I don't know. Em, how could I know anything? I'm winging this too."

"She asked a stranger on the internet to take her. Amy too!" Didn't dad see how dangerous this situation had become. Mom was like a ticking time bomb and we didn't know when she was going to explode, or combust. Or what?!

"I don't know what else to do. I can't put her in a cage. I'm terrified she's going to get hurt...or worse." Dad mumbled more to himself as he went inside.

I sat outside staring at the truck. Trying to think of what on earth I could do to wake up my mom and end this madness. My feelings were swishing around in my chest; euphoria over the way my relationship with José was developing and sadness over my mom's mental decline. I felt helpless along with slightly irked. With everything bubbling up to the surface, the end result left me totally and completely seasick.

CHAPTER THIRTY-TWO

I downloaded a sound maker app to Nora's phone so she could listen to the ocean waves. Amy was at dance class, so I gave my mom a jar of coconut oil to slather all over herself and asked her to please stay in her room while I worked on my very important English project.

"With José?" she asked.

"Yes."

"Is he your boyfriend officially yet?"

"Um, no. It's still TBD. There are a few…obstacles." I hated that he had a girlfriend, even if she wasn't really his girlfriend. I was so tired of being a secret, exacerbated by the pure exhaustion of having my mother believe she is a mermaid.

Nora shut the laptop next to her on the bed and my instincts caught on fire. What was she up to this time?

"Are you trying to find someone online to drive you to the Pacific Ocean again? Are you in contact with the BigDaddy number guy again? I swear to God, Nora, I will lose it!"

"No," She patted the bed for me to sit by her and opened the lap top. She had been shopping for more shell crowns on

Etsy. Wonderful, she'd have a massive collection soon. But at least my heart rate slowed down. "You, Janet, and Bart have made it very clear that there are predators online that would take advantage of me."

"Okay. Good." At least I could trust that she adhered to safety precautions. Thankfully, my mermaid mother still had some common sense.

"But honestly, Emily. I don't know what the fuss is all about. Catfish can't type."

So much for my common sense argument. There was no point explaining that catfished was a verb based off of an MTV show that exposed online frauds.

"Okay, Nora. Just stay offline. Please."

"If it makes you happy. I just want you to be happy. You know that, right?!" She looked at me with such hopeful eyes. So sweet and innocent.

"Yes, Nora. I do know that." And I wanted to believe her, but I wasn't happy.

In fact, I was irate and my stomach gurgled with anxiety. It was time for José and I to have a real conversation about our relationship status. He couldn't just keep me on the back burner and think I was going to be okay with it. I was not that kind of girl. That kind being a floozy.

I had made my mind up. Two things needed to happen;

1. José had to break it off with Savannah publicly.
2. We had to make our relationship official.

The inner-turmoil was just too much for me to take any longer.

I took a few deep breaths when he knocked on the door. "I'll leave you two alone," Nora said, her focus returned to the display of shell crowns of every color.

"Hey," I exhaled as I opened the door.

José was reading something on his phone, and held up his finger to signal he needed a sec. I stood in the doorway, watching him type something and then tuck his phone into his back pocket.

"Hey, yourself," he said and he swooped in for a kiss, pressing me against the wood frame, kissing me as we backed into the living room. Somehow, I closed the front door and we separated our lips long enough to set his backpack on a chair by the table. We each took a seat.

"What's up?" José asked, "Everything okay?"

I nodded. I didn't want to attack him the second he came in the door, right after he'd kissed me like he needed my lips to live.

"Okay, let's do this." He opened his backpack and scattered his books and binders around, picking his favorite pen from his pencil case.

He didn't seem to be the slightest bit worried about our relationship, or the fact that no one knew about our relationship, but us, and a mermaid. Not even Kessia, which was basically breaking every friend code rule ever.

I started a mental mantra, telling myself over and over that I had to be strong. As much as I wanted to be with José, I wasn't being true to myself.

We worked on our English project in silence for awhile, each lost in our own thoughts. He'd tap my toe and smile at me when I looked up at him, and then we'd go back to deciphering what on earth Shakespeare was saying.

He leaned in and kissed me.

As much as I wanted to lose myself in the escape of his lips, I couldn't. I sat up straighter and tilted my head to the side, thinking of how I was going to present my testimony to him. I had to make sure I didn't come off as manipulative or having a self-serving agenda. I just needed to be real and speak my truth. It was now or never.

"When are you breaking it off with Savannah?"

"Savannah is always going to be in my life, Emily." His pen flew into his mouth and he started gnawing on the end of it.

"Yes, I mean, okay. I get it, she's family. But when are you going to break up with her? I mean, for real. With everyone knowing?"

"Why? Don't you trust me?" He slammed the pen on the table and looked at me like I had stabbed him in the heart, or at least a major artery.

"Of course, I do. I really do. I have to or I couldn't do this," I pointed to myself and then him, and then back to myself.

"I like you, Emily. That should be enough."

"I don't want to be a secret," I said, trying not to cry.

"If you don't trust me, we don't have a relationship."

How did this get turned around on me? I wasn't the one with a boyfriend everyone thought I was dating. I hadn't done anything wrong, had I? Well, that probably depended on knowing all the facts and intentions. All I knew was that I was not prepared for this emotional tennis match.

José got up to leave. "Trust is everything to me."

Nora entered the room without my noticing, until a cloud of glitter erupted. She blew it out of her hand and it landed over us. Glitter was everywhere; clinging to our skin and falling into puddles on our shoes.

"Nora!" I yelled, brushing the glitter from my hair.

I looked at José. He was even more handsome with glitter on his face. Glistening freckles accentuated his nose and cheeks.

"It's a mermaid blessing," she enlightened us. "So, you'll be happy forever."

While I was dying inside, José was his most charming. He hugged Nora, thanking her for the blessing.

"I think it worked," he said. "I'm happy. Emily, are you?"

In that moment, I was. Oddly, the glitter bomb had erased my venom.

José pulled me in for an unexpected hug. I closed my eyes and savored the moment. I didn't know how many more I had with him. How many I'd allow myself to have. He held me for a few extra seconds, and then released me. Was glitter an aphrodisiac?

"Are you ready for a swim?" I asked Nora, hoping she'd slip away and give me a moment to swallow José's face before he left. And to my good fortune, she disappeared long enough to let my lips show him how happy I was.

CHAPTER THIRTY-THREE

While reading a text, I almost fell into the pool at the Y, walking dangerously close to the deep end. "Whooh," I recovered myself. Although I had a Lifeproof case on my phone, I'd have to implement a no walking and texting rule. Even my cell phone case was responsible like me, instead of a cute fashion statement.

The pool was way more crowded than usual, with bobs of hair, and glimpses of color popping in-and-out of the pool.

Was that a tail?

It was. A mermaid tail. And another one. I counted eight, shiny, shimmery, rainbow hued tails flapping around in the water.

Tia stood on the sideline, a clipboard in her hand. She instructed the women on what to do next. "Ladies, hold onto the side of the pool and swish your tail in front of you. Yes, like that Maribelle."

As I approached her, I realized her t-shirt read, *Mermaid Trainer.*

"Hi Emily, your mom is in the locker room."

"What's going on?" I asked, pointing to the pool.

"Some of the women wanted to be mermaids too. Kind of like a support group, and I think some of them just wanted to be mermaids. So, the Y started a new type of workout class." She looked back and forth from me to the pool while she talked.

"Ridiculous," I huffed. Each colorful tail was like a knife to my heart, a betrayal of sorts.

"It's my most popular session now. We started a few weeks ago and it keeps growing." Tia was obviously not aware that this news was like someone lit the fuse to my cannon.

"It's not funny. My mom isn't a joke!" I blasted into the air. "She's sick, really sick...and you're making money off her. How could you?"

"Emily, no one here is laughing at your mom. I promise you," Tia reached out and put her hand on my shoulder. "They get it. In fact, they get it more than anyone."

"What does that even mean? How could they get it? Because I don't get it at all! I don't understand where my mother's memory went or why her entire world has become a mythological story," I ranted by the side of the pool, not caring that the guests who walked past us were staring at me, the girl having a meltdown outside the mermaid swim class. "I don't get what is going on in her head and it scares me to death. So please, Tia, enlighten me."

"These women are overworked, underpaid, spread way too thin with families, volunteering, cooking, cleaning, and everything else women are expected to do. All while trying to look like a supermodel. Women need a break. I'm doing a project for school on it now. I'm calling it, *The Mermaid Phenomenon.*" Tia began to explain, but my brain wasn't completely absorbing it. I was bent, but I couldn't pinpoint why. These women weren't doing anything malicious, but I was personally insulted and ashamed for my mom. She was having some sort of mental crisis, not a masquerade ball.

"Emily, your mother has been doing it all for years, and she was...is...mentally exhausted. These women are not making fun of her. They're supporting her," Tia bent over and helped a woman adjust the waist band of her tail. She returned to where I was standing and continued, "I know this is hard for you. It's extremely stressful, and confusing, and...complicated."

I was confused. Everything in my own mind was fuzzy and disoriented, like I didn't know which end was up.

"Remember I told you about unconventional grief. I really think you should talk to a professional. And a support group can be lifesaving."

"A support group? Really? There are more people whose mothers think they're mermaids!?! Fan-freaken-tastic!" I was making a scene. I knew I was and it was like my rage was exploding out of me and I couldn't stop it. I didn't care who was watching.

"Emily, you have to take care of yourself during this situation. Your mother needs you, but you have to take care of you, too," Tia instructed, pointing her finger all the way to my chest and lightly touching me above my heart. Honestly, I didn't even know what she meant. How did I take care of myself when that's what my mother used to do? And I didn't even really know how to take care of her. I was improvising and pretty much failing.

"I'm not sure," I thought out loud, realizing I had been standing there like a statue, planted firmly in that exact spot, not ready to physically move.

"I have some brochures for you; they're in my car. I found a place that has support groups for family members," Tia informed me. "You should go."

"Any brochures on how to care for a mermaid?" I sort of joked, but there was too much truth in that statement for it to be labeled as amusing. I felt like a car that was out of gas.

Nora came blasting out of the locker room and jumped into the pool, a perfect cannonball.

"Nora, no running. You know the rules," Tia scolded after blowing her whistle in my ear.

"I'm sorry, Tia. I just love my legs!" My mother shouted in return.

"Nora the Mermaid," the women cheered for her.

Nora swam over and greeted me. "Hi Emily, get in!"

"I'll wait on the bench," I answered, finally able to move from my spot by the pool, though my feet felt like they were full of sand.

Too annoyed to concentrate on my homework, I watched the women enjoy their mermaid class. It was a diverse group of all ages, all sizes, and all colors of skin. Oddly, my mom was the only one NOT wearing a mermaid tail, but she seemed thrilled that the other women were. In fact, she helped them with their swimming and gave advice on how to get out of the pool gracefully.

Nora spewed facts as if she was an oceanographer, talking about evil sunscreen that was killing off their coral and how the oil spill of 2010 affected her personally. She was so convincing, I almost believed her traumatic story of escaping the devastation by holding onto an unsuspecting fishing boat until she was out of danger.

Before each woman got out of the pool, Tia asked them a question and filmed their answer on her phone.

"What does being a mermaid mean to you?"

"Escape from my real life," a woman adorning a hot pink tail answered. Adding, "which is boring AF."

"I'm sexy and powerful!" a plump, newly converted mermaid purred.

"My childhood. I feel young," a lovely green-tailed clad, but wrinkled woman responded, her voice raspy as if she'd smoked cigarettes for seventy years.

The answers penetrated my skull. Why did these women all want to live different lives? What was so bad about theirs that they looked for an escape? Were all women over thirty miserable?

Kessia and I texted until Nora and part of her mermaid

posse poured out of the locker room, chatting and glowing from their workout. Mom appeared so much younger, still wearing her braids, all smiling and laughing with the other ladies.

She never used to smile when she volunteered at my elementary school. Not Nora. She was too preoccupied with her work to let her hair down. I remember it always being pulled back tight in a bun. I always knew she wanted to be a part of my life and did her best to actively participate in class parties with the other moms, but I could tell my childhood events were keeping her from more important matters. I used to wish she'd be one of the PTA moms who cut loose and had a dance party, and here she was, with a gaggle of women, as if she didn't have a care in the world.

"I'll need you all to sign permission wavers for my class," Tia informed them. "It's completely optional. Don't feel pressured to participate if you're not comfortable with my professor seeing you in your tail."

Thanks to Nora's horrific storytelling, I had nightmares all night about being caught in an oil spill. I was under the water, unable to swim because of a bright, orange fin binding my legs together. And I choked on thick, black liquid until it pulled me completely under into nothingness.

CHAPTER THIRTY-FOUR

L ooking out my window, I could see Kessia in Fred's backyard and she wasn't alone. A muscular farmer was shoveling what appeared to be piles of pig poop from Nora's latest animal additions. He was wearing overalls, work boots, and a straw hat. Kessia worked to attach a barrier to the side of the fence, creating shade for the newly-relocated, swine family.

Scrounging for some clean clothes that sort of matched, I raced downstairs to find a beverage to bring over. We were out of lemonade. And well, everything, so I made a pitcher of ice water and grabbed some glasses, shoving on flip-flops on my way out the door.

Fred was on the porch, a chicken in his lap, "Zoo's always open, Darlin'."

"Good morning, Fred," I rushed, cutting through his house and out the back.

As I came closer to the farmer I concluded it was Stud Muffin Jack himself, and he was dripping in sweat.

"Hey Jack," I called out, holding up the water.

Kessia and Jack circled me, taking the water greedily.

"We needed a break," Kessia started.

"Yeah, that Shakespeare stuff is mind numbing," Jack added.

"How are you guys doing? With your project and all, I mean?"

"I'm following Kessia's lead." He pointed to her head. "She seems to have it all worked out in there."

"Yes, it's all in here," she patted his back.

He picked up the shovel and went back to work, clearing a path. The pigs curled up in the shade, watching him like we were.

She leaned towards me, pointed to her head and whispered, "It's so not in here."

I motioned to Kessia, mouthing, O. M. G.

"I know. Jack's clearing up the pig mess for Fred." Kessia smiled and bit her lip.

Jack was working his butt off while Kessia and I rested against the fence.

"He's doing it for you," I said.

"Nah, he needed to move. The sitting around reading was killing him."

"Kessia, he's cleaning up pig doo-doo for you. Don't you get it? He likes you." My words gently smacking upside the head.

"Shut up!" She looked shocked, "He does not."

"He does."

"Yeah, my dad liked my mom once." Kessia looked away from Jack, possibly seeing their entire teen romance play out in her head, ending with Kessia alone and Jack with a younger woman.

"He probably never shoveled manure for her. That's love," I said, making a heart with my hands.

Though she smiled again, she shook off the thought, "Not happening."

"I love him," I sighed.

"Stop," she put her walls up higher, blocking me with her hand.

"My parents won't make me come clean these pig pens. Who do you think is going to have to shovel pig poop if Jack doesn't? I'm not kidding. I love him." I meant it. I loved that he was doing my new, unwanted chores.

She tried to put her hand over my mouth. "Shhhhh. He'll hear you."

"I love you, Jack," I yelled.

He turned and gave me a grin and got back to work.

"I mean it," I yelled some more.

Kessia ducked behind a plant as red as the flowers in bloom. She jumped up, knocking me into the plant too.

"I love you!" I hollered, as she sacked me, both of us covered in dirt, and leaves, and most likely bugs.

"I'm a mess," I laughed, once the wind returned to my lungs.

"People pay a lot of money for this kind of natural exfoliation," Kessia stated.

"Yeah, well, I've got a pile that Jack's made if they want the full organic experience."

"We could charge people to visit Fred's." Kessia thought out loud as we lay in the dirt. "Like a petting zoo for kids…and a spa for adults."

I mulled it over, wondering if the idea was genius, preposterous, or a combination of both. Regardless, Kessia was destined to be a business mogul, and I still had to figure out what to do with the rest of my life.

"Want to go out with Benny?" she asked.

"Not a chance. I have him in history and he acts twelve." I left out that Benny constantly made mermaid jokes about my mother during class, knowing Kessia would kill him on my behalf and I couldn't lose my best friend right now.

"Yeah, an immature twelve. But he's Jack's best friend, so I thought we could all go out. Like a group thing." So, Kessia was warming to Jack, just not ready to jump in. But I couldn't sacrifice myself to Benny no matter how much I wanted Kessia and Jack's love to bloom.

"Not gonna happen. Ever." I spoke in my low, serious voice so she would know there was no room to negotiate.

"You still holding out for Savannah to fall off the face of earth?" She inquired, a totally fair question.

I shrugged. I guess I was. And Kessia had no idea how badly I hoped that would happen.

CHAPTER THIRTY-FIVE

I had to be at José's by sunset and it was the first time I was dreading seeing him. In my mind fog of anger, I forgot to arrange for Kessia to pick up Nora, who had a late swim session. Dad had a dullsville insurance convention in Lincoln, but promised he would come home even if it ended late, rather than sleep over. Even so, I was technically on mermaid duty, but I was too furious to think straight.

If José wasn't going to share our relationship openly with everyone at school, then I was not going to spend any more time with him. Other than our English project, obviously, so it really wouldn't be that much time together, and in reality, we could work separately and compare notes. Not that José had any notes; I hadn't seen him write one thing down since we started.

I threw a barrette that was falling out of my hair and grunted, "How could I be so stupid?!"

I just couldn't stand the feeling of being the other woman. Like a mistress or something. I couldn't shake feeling dishonorable. Even though I didn't necessarily like Savannah, I didn't want to hurt her. And I didn't want any detrimental relationship karma hanging over my head.

José was waiting out front when I arrived, looking all handsome and perfect. I dug deep for my self-respect and promised myself I wouldn't cave to the tenderness of his lips.

"We need to talk," I began.

"Okay," he said. "First, I want to show you something."

He led me around the side of his house, opening the gate. As we passed through, I noticed rose petals on the ground. Dead roses, I told myself. I would not give up my morals because he scattered potpourri.

We followed the trail of flowers to a make-shift drive in theater. José had set up a movie screen outside, with a projector attached to his computer. There were blankets and tons of pillows surrounding lawn furniture. Sparkling lights twinkled on the fence, spelling out my name.

"I used wire coat hangers," he boasted, chest inflated and proud of his own skills. "Do you like it?"

Before I could answer, he revealed a heart, made from another coat hanger, wrapped in blinking red lights.

He motioned for me to sit down in the cozy cove he had created.

"I want you to know how much I like you."

"José…"

"I know it's been hard with my situation, and you've been so understanding and patient."

"Not really," I said honestly.

But I loved the heart. It blinked in my hands, radiating how I felt.

"They're battery lights. You don't have to plug them in."

"I really hate your Savannah situation," I held strong. Barely.

"I know," he was so close I could smell his skin. He was wearing cologne. "I'm just asking for a little more time."

Without waiting for my response, he pushed play, and an old black and white movie appeared on the screen. I lost myself in the movie and snuggled as close to José as two people could be without being conjoined twins.

José... he made my name in lights and coat hangers, with a heart.

I was weak.

We didn't talk much during the entire movie, which was rare for us. Instead, we just breathed together, and as Tia would say, exchanged neurons.

The stars held our attention as we lay light-years away.

José rolled over and faced me, "If you had to live in the black and white movie days or now, which would you pick?"

"Now." Duh, right now. Like this very second now. I wanted to stop time and live in this moment forever.

"One of the guys who invented Twitter is from a farm in Nebraska," José said, staring at the stars.

I'd heard that. Or read about him somewhere.

"Yeah. Do you want to be famous? For inventing a car design or a part or something?" I asked, wondering how on earth you invent Twitter from Nebraska.

"Nah. Would be cool, I guess, but not a goal." He turned to me and smiled, and though I had the constellations above me, his mouth was more beautiful than the big dipper, and slightly the same shape. When he spoke, his lips opened wider on one side and then formed a curved line on the other side. And when his lips pressed against mine, it was like being kissed by a star.

We stayed there for hours. Talking, laughing, and I think I even cried a little bit. I was definitely a teenager in love for the first time. Whether it was right or wrong, it just was. Earth stopped spinning for a little while and it was only José and I. Like *Romeo and Juliet*, destined to be together, or at least that's what I told myself.

When I finally checked my phone, I was bombarded by a million texts from Dad. I was in so much trouble. Not only had I revolted against my own code of common decency, I'd completely forgotten to pick up my mom.

CHAPTER THIRTY-SIX

The house was dark except the porch light. I walked as slowly as I could to the door and entered, knowing I was about to get blasted. Dad was waiting in the living room, lit by a single lamp that made the glitter splattering on the wall more prominent.

"I'm sorry; I know I messed up." I waved the white flag, trying to deflate Dad's anger before he lashed out, but my attempt failed.

"I can't believe you forgot your mother!" Dad said in a harsh whisper, trying to get his point across, without waking Amy.

"She forgot my entire existence."

"Emily, I'm so disappointed in you."

In that moment, I didn't care. I had the best night of my life and I wasn't going to let Nora ruin it. Not tonight. The red coat hanger heart flashed in my hands.

"I'm not one hundred percent sure what irony is, but I'm guessing this is ironic."

"That's enough," he shouted, then lowered his voice. "She was really upset, Emily. Your mom is scared..."

"She was with Tia. It isn't like I left her stranded in the desert." I hated that my mother was frightened. She was scared of everything now and it activated a steady anxiety in me. What if I couldn't make it in the world? What if it's much scarier out there than I ever imagined? My entire universe was out of control.

"Emily, you knew I was at a conference. I couldn't just leave," he explained as if I didn't know. He was always at a conference. He never could leave. Nora was my responsibility, but it was too much to carry on my own.

"Yeah, well, I can't just stop living my life either!" I kicked the bottom of the couch and had the strong urge to scream.

I took a few deep breaths to calm myself. It's going to be okay, I told myself. I can figure it out. I'll try harder. "Okay. I'll talk to the school about staying home. Maybe getting my work in advance. Summer's only a few weeks…"

Dad cut me off, "Your grandmother is coming…"

"You called her to babysit me! I'm sixteen-years-old." I retreated from the living room and stormed down the hall to my room. Dad followed.

"She can help with Amy. And Nora," he stated. "Em, I get that you need help here. I need it too."

"She doesn't even like mom!"

I slammed my door, completely forgetting about my sleeping sister.

"You're grounded, young lady," Dad said from outside my door.

"Yeah, I'm grounded. But I'm still her personal taxi driver!" I yelled before sticking in my headphones and blasting my music. The red heart José gave me blinked on and off, as if accentuating the song that vibrated in my ears. We had managed the last few weeks without help. So what if I messed up one time!? I'm a teenager. I'm not perfect. I'm not supposed to be. But, now I was getting a babysitter and it was so insulting.

As the anger evaporated, the fear kicked in. What if mom

had been hurt? What if my mom had died? Or was going to die? What if she left to find the Pacific Ocean on a train? Or a bus? And I never saw her again.

Once fear was done dancing around in my head for what seemed like forever, shame arrived.

And the truth was, I had failed Nora. All I had to do was pick her up and I forgot. Even though she thought she was a mermaid, she was still my mother. No one was more disappointed at me than myself.

CHAPTER THIRTY-SEVEN

Determined and on a covert mission, I guided Nora into Dr. Sy's waiting room early. We sat in the chairs side-by-side. Neither of us wanted to color. Nora sulked, staring longingly out the window.

"What's the matter?"

She forced a smile and patted my leg, "I'm fine."

I hated when people said they were fine when clearly they weren't. Here she was wearing a shell crown, her hair a million pastels, she couldn't do her job, or drive, and she was 'fine.'

"Yeah, you're fine all right," I checked the time on my phone again. Where was Dr. Sy? She was four minutes late and I was fuming.

"I miss my home," she sighed. "And...my friends."

"Your family?" I asked, with sarcasm and vitriol.

"Yes, my family," she continued to stare out the window.

I stood up and let the emotions explode out of me, "Why are Amy and I not enough for you? Why aren't we worth fighting for? Why?"

Nora looked at me as if I'd hit her. She shrunk away from me.

"Why am I not worth waking up for?" I cried.

Dr. Sy opened the door and greeted us. "Sorry, I'm late Nora. I had a client emergency."

"It's all right," Nora said, walking into her office. Dr. Sy looked at me, reading my face, and possibly my mind. "Are you okay, Emily?"

"FIX HER!" I shouted, way too loud for an office building, and ran down the hall.

CHAPTER THIRTY-EIGHT

H*i, it's Tia, can you pick me up? Your mom gave me your number.*
I pulled over while driving, parked, and then read the text; slightly bummed it wasn't from José.

I responded yes and she sent her address. Of course I would help Tia. I liked her and she was good to my mom.

GPS landed me at a dilapidated apartment complex in a desolate part of town I had never been too. I parked and then meandered around until I found apartment 4-C and knocked.

Tia opened the door.

"Thanks for getting me. My clunker died."

"Happy to help." I wiped my feet on the welcome mat.

"Come, meet Polly." I followed her through the sparsely decorated living room to a bedroom. A frail woman with a turban on her head, rested against a pillow, her feet elevated, covered in cozy socks.

"Hello," I greeted her. "It's nice to meet you."

Polly attempted to talk, but it proved too much.

"Just rest," Tia soothed her. "Emily's giving me a ride. I'll be back early tonight."

She kissed her on the forehead and we left, Tia locking the front door behind us.

"Cancer," she announced and I knew she was referring to Polly.

"I'm so sorry. Is she your mom?" I asked, treading lightly and not wanting to upset Tia.

"Yes, my foster. Adoption never went through. My real mom kept fighting it." She sighed, "My biological mom."

"Oh." I hated that I sounded stupid, but I didn't know what to say.

"I aged out of the system, but Polly's my real family," she smiled and it seemed she was comforting me instead of the other way around. Darn it, I was friend failing. "Yeah. When Polly got sick a few years ago, I figured I better hurry up and get my life jump started. Got my GED and started college. Work when I can, help Polly the rest of the time."

I followed her to the parking lot, and waited while she collected her stuff out of her car. The door creaked and I thought it might fall off the hinges. I was embarrassed that I had complained about my manual car windows when my engine was fairly new.

"Gonna tow it?" I inquired, assuming she had Triple A or car insurance for times like this. Nora had always prepared us for emergencies. "Here's your Triple A card, Emily. Keep it handy in your wallet. They'll tow you to the closest station within seven miles." I hadn't even had to think about it. Or prepare. I had Triple A, thanks to Nora.

"I'll have to tow it. Directly to the junkyard, I guess. I'll notify you of the funeral service." Tia joked about the situation, most likely to keep from crying.

"No way to fix it?" I crossed my fingers and toes that it was savable.

"In lieu of flowers, please send all donations directly to me."

We laughed at the catastrophe that was her dying car and I was glad I could give her a ride, but wished I could do more.

"It would cost more than the car is worth to fix." She exhaled, "I have money saved for a new one. A new-*used* one."

"Oh good." At least it sounded good to me.

"Yeah, I was hoping to use it for school, but I need the transportation. That's life."

As we drove off, I asked, "Is she getting better? Polly, I mean."

"Yes. She just had surgery, which set her back, but full recovery expected." Tia organized her bag while she spoke. "Cancer sucks, in case you didn't know."

"What about your real mom? Do you mind me asking?" Maybe it was because my mom was ill, but I was curious.

"My childhood was hell on earth. I'm like a Phoenix, rising up from the ashes, and I'm not waiting on anyone to forge my path." She tucked a swimsuit into the side of her bag, "Polly's my real mom."

"Inspiring. You know, Nora...my mom...she has helped a lot of people." I thought about the person Nora used to be.

"I know," Tia responded as we pulled into the Y parking lot, "I'm one of them."

Wow. Nora had helped Tia.

"I can give you a ride anytime," I offered.

"No worries, my bus pass should get me through the week." She held up her fist and smiled at me, before disappearing into the sports club.

I didn't even know Columbus had a bus. Maybe Janet was right, I was sheltered. How was I completely oblivious to public transportation? How much else did I take completely for granted? Am I horrible person and had absolutely no idea?

CHAPTER THIRTY-NINE

G ran had never been conservative, or traditional for that matter. While Nora was the Queen-of-Rules, dad's mother was the polar opposite, so it wasn't surprising that they had never gotten along. Nora couldn't handle the disarray that is Gran's life, and Gran detested Nora's rigidness and rules. *"There is no right way,"* Gran would argue to Nora's deaf ears.

The royal purple hair style Gran arrived with would have been more dramatic if Nora, Kessia and Amy didn't have a rainbow of extensions. Gran was probably expecting some kind of shock and awe reaction to her violet dyed hue, but that had become pretty standard in our house.

"I was inspired by the poem *When I am Old I Shall Wear Purple,*" she explained, running her fingers through her short, spiky lavender puff.

"It looks like cotton candy," Amy hugged her. "I love it!"

"Or a bridge troll," Dad commented.

It was no wonder why Dad married someone more stable and reserved as Nora pre-mermaid incident. He seemed to want Gran to be some version of Martha Stewart, but without the whole jail thing. But Gran, was Gran, and I absolutely adored her and the way life became a roller coaster when she was around.

"So what was her crime?" Gran gave me her best stern look while directing her question to Dad. She started ripping off her own answers, guessing what I had done.

"Tramp stamp on her backside? I got my first tattoo when I was 15...in Bali."

"No."

"Lewd and disorderly conduct in public? I'll plead the fifth on that one...and I'd have to plead it a few times. Skinny dipping and all."

Dad shook his head no and exhaled a massive amount of annoyance.

"Oh good Heavens, she's pregnant!" Gran beamed. No doubt, envisioning herself with a baby car seat on the back of a motorcycle.

"She forgot her mother," Dad cut her off.

"Huh?"

"Emily was supposed to pick her mother up from the Y, and she forgot. Nora was stuck there for hours."

"So she was a teenager?" Gran questioned, clearly not on the same page as Dad.

"She was responsible for her mother's well-being. Nora is ..."

Nora smiled from the corner, stepping over to Gran and giving her a big hug. Her shell crown spent a few moments tangled in Gran's purple puff. Amy and I exchanged an amused glance.

"Gran, it's so nice to finally meet you. Bart the Pirate has told me so many wonderful things about you."

They looked like two cartoon characters with their bright hair.

"I'm Nora. Nora the Mermaid."

I could have sworn I saw a twinkle in Gran's eye, "Oh, this is going to be a hoot."

CHAPTER FORTY

A my and Gran played Go Fish at the kitchen table.
"What else she got?" Gran asked, digging for scoop
on Nora's mermaid maladies.

"She gets distracted easily by things. Like sparkles." Amy
examined her cards for matches, "Or glitter."

"Shiny Object Syndrome," Gran concluded.

"That's a real thing?" I asked. Would that info be useful for
my case? Would Gran make an expert witness?

"Yes. Not real like a medical diagnosis, but a real symptom."

Nothing in this house was real. It was like living in a matrix.
I yanked the cereal out of the pantry, spilling it all over the floor.

"Gran, did you bring my birth video?"

"I thought you were joking. Why on earth would anyone
want to see that? I threw that out when I moved from Tuba City
to Roswell. Or maybe it melted in that house fire when I lived in
Baltimore."

"Gran! I really needed that. I need proof that Nora is my
mother."

"Our mother," Amy echoed.

"That video would have been irrefutable." I had to bite my lip so tears didn't flood from my eyes.

"You okay, Lovey?" Gran asked.

"She doesn't seem to be getting better. It's like she wants to stay a mermaid forever."

"Yeah," Amy agreed. "I miss mom."

"Really?" Gran joked. Or maybe she wasn't joking. "I like the mermaid."

"You're welcome to drive her around town."

"I'll pass, Sweetheart. You just got your license; it's good practice for ya. I've been driving for a gazillion years. My feet are tired."

"Okay, Gran. See you guys later."

Yeah, I was grounded-ish, but since Dad had become a single parent, I was learning the beauty and manipulation of outnumbering the power unit. Honestly, there was really no way for Dad to follow through on his punishment. He needed my help, which tipped the scale in my favor. I almost felt sorry for him, but not enough to discipline myself. No one is that good.

Janet had texted earlier, wanting me to stop by and pick up some items for Nora. We left early so Nora wouldn't be late for swim.

Child Protective Services was on the far side of town, towards Tia's apartments. The building had cracks and needed a paint job, but the government didn't waste a lot of money on maintenance. As we pulled up to my mom's previous place of employment, Nora shrank away from the car door.

"Janet's waiting," I pleaded, trying to get her to come in with me.

"I can't go in there," she cried.

After five minutes of begging for her to at least wait on the steps, I locked her in the car and ran inside. She was worse than a toddler because I couldn't physically pick her up, place her on my hip, and get things done.

Security checked me in, announcing my arrival to Janet.

"You know where she is?" the security guard asked.

"Yes, I think so," although I hadn't been there in a while, mom had worked there my entire life, so I was familiar with her office and the layout.

Janet was at her desk on the phone. She held up a finger, motioning for me to wait.

Since I had to pee so bad my stomach hurt, I grabbed the women's bathroom key and headed down the hall. Finding one of the bathrooms open, I went in and sat on the toilet, taking in my surroundings.

For the first time, I realized there was a shower in there. Hotel sized bottles of shampoo and conditioner were piled in a basket. Boxes of different feminine hygiene products lined the counter, but the boxes were all empty. A sign on the wall read, "Ask your service coordinator for a razor."

Janet was waiting for me in the hallway when I came out.

"I have one bag that needs to be refrigerated asap. And another that goes into the pantry. No sun," she purged.

"Why would anyone ask for a razor?" I asked.

"Some people don't have anywhere to shower, Emily," she wasn't condescending, for once. "There are runaways, mostly from abusive families, that only shower once a week. Or sometimes an entire month. We don't leave razors out or they'll take the whole box."

"Oh." I hadn't realized. My mom had worked there forever and I never put it all together.

Janet continued as we entered her office. "Same with the tampons, but we're more lenient with those. People steal those because they need them. The shampoo's donated, but the towels are gone too. Sometimes I feel like a concierge."

"Mom's waiting in the car," I said, soaking in the despair of the place. No wonder Nora wouldn't come inside.

"I'll take these out to her," she referred to the bags. "Do me a favor and load the tampons for me."

I reluctantly grabbed a handful of tampons and made my

way back to the bathroom, examining the walls like a detective, searching for clues of my mother's pre-mermaid life. There were pictures of smiling families, some interracial, and company picnics with balloons and cake. Celebrations amongst the disasters.

Though I knew I shouldn't, I meandered into my mom's office. Maybe there was something there I could use to trigger mom's memory, or at least some evidence for my case to prove she is my mother.

The office was frozen in time; papers peppered the desk, her stapler, a collection of pens. A collage of photos hung on the wall; Amy and me, her and Bart, the entire family. It was like looking at pictures of someone else's family, a family I knew once a long, long time ago. Would Nora ever return to work here? Would I ever see my real mom again? Forcing back tears, I retreated back to the hallway.

Not looking where I was going, I bumped into someone. "Sorry," I said, noting the teenage girl looked familiar. I was pretty sure she went to my school, but I didn't know her. Her hair needed washing and her clothes were dirty.

"What are you doing here?" she asked, looking down.

"Oh," I answered. "Putting these back. My service coordinator said I couldn't keep them all. Stingy bitches," I added for effect.

Her lips cracked slightly, "Yeah, bitches."

She watched me cram the tampons into an open box. I fumbled with them nervously, wanting to get out of her way so she could clean up.

"They're kind of nice, I guess." I lied; Janet had never been nice to me. "They let us keep the towels."

"Yeah," she barely mumbled.

"See ya around," I waved as I exited, closing the door behind me. Leaving her in peace.

"Bitches?" Janet smirked as I passed her in the hall.

"I freaked."

"Thanks, Emily."

A genuine thank you, not the usual sarcastic Janet, making it clear I was beneath her. But a real thank you. I didn't know if it was for picking up my mom's stuff, or for not embarrassing the teenage girl. My emotions were stirring like a volcano in my stomach and I was worried I was close to blowing.

I breathed a sigh of relief when I saw Nora still in the car, exactly where I left her. I stared at her for a moment, trying to see my old mom. The mom that worked at Child Protective Services and didn't dress like a mermaid. Who was she? Who is she now? And did I ever really know my mother before the accident at all?

CHAPTER FORTY-ONE

Nora livened up as she swam, the pool being her magical elixir. Her and the rest of the mermaids sloshed around in a euphoric daze, spinning and swooshing through their imaginary sea. They looked like they were having the time of their lives. Maybe they were.

Splash!

The water was crisp, my body languid, as I fell into the deep end, sinking slowly. My shirt bunched up at my middle, and my skirt danced around me like a jellyfish, flashing my blue Monday underwear that covered more than my swimsuit bottoms. Releasing my toes, my flip-flops buoyed to the surface like cannons.

I sensed all eyes were on me and I was surrounded by mermaid tails.

Using my legs, I blasted out of the water, catching my breath before torpedoing into my own lane and I started to swim. Far reaching arm strokes powered through the liquid and washed away my stress, cleansing my hypothalamus — my brain's emotional control center, I recalled from a science lesson. My body needed this. I kicked my legs as hard as I could, until I was physically spent.

And then I switched to the breast stroke. Bobbing in and out of the water like a frog.

I needed this. I so needed to move. The H2O. The aquatic therapy. Everything.

When I was out of breath, I took a break at the edge of the pool. Everything hurt. My lungs were begging for air, my muscles awake.

Nora swam up beside me. "Feels good, doesn't it?"

"Amazing."

We were finally bonding over something just as Amy had done. We floated together for awhile, feeling both refreshed and exhausted.

Tia offered me two towels as I climbed out of the pool. "One to dry off and one for your car ride home."

"Thanks."

"How's your project? *The Mermaid Phenomenon?*" I asked, wringing out my shirt.

"Almost done. Editing in the final clips. It's pretty good, if I do say so myself. And I do. Loudly." She boasted in a good way. Confident, not narcissistic.

"That's great."

"So, you gonna start swimming with the ladies?"

"Maybe." I definitely was, but I'd bring my swimsuit next time. "I think Nora would be happy to know she's still helping people, even if she's not coherent enough to know it."

"Yeah, I think you're right." Tia smiled.

I hurried home to transform myself into something presentable for José. It was our last movie night and I wanted Nora tucked away with Dad, so I didn't get myself into any more trouble.

Still giddy from my swim, I jumped into the shower, wondering what on earth José would surprise me with next.

CHAPTER FORTY-TWO

Skipping up to José's porch, I rang the doorbell, slightly saddened that José wasn't outside waiting to greet me as usual. Yes, I saw José at school yesterday, but still, a warm welcome was always appreciated. And hugs and kisses were nice, too.

Savannah opened the door. "Hey, Emily. So, English project...still."

"Yeah."

"Come in." She held the door open, her hands turned up like a hostess of a gameshow. "Please remove your shoes."

I followed Savannah through the entry and into the open kitchen-living room area.

We joined a fiesta already in action.

Tasha and Amelia were busy setting out a taco bar; mountains of fresh guacamole and salsa were in black pots on the counter. The blender whirred out a mix of tequila and limes, and the *Gypsy Kings* blared from indoor speakers.

"I can't believe you guys are still doing this English project," Amelia started. "Don't you have other classes and things to do? Estupido."

"We turned in our project last week," Savannah bragged. "It's not like it was hard or anything."

José rolled his eyes, "Whatever, genius," and grabbed a handful of tortilla chips. "Emily's got it all worked out."

What? When did this become my project and José was only along for the ride?

"Which Universities are you applying too?" Tasha asked me. She looked more like Savannah's sister than her mother, but only because of her inappropriate clothing choices and their matching spray tans.

"I'm not sure yet."

"Oh, well, which major? That always narrows down the search."

"The last quiz I did said I'd be good at Russian Studies, Sports Business, and Human Resources. I'm still not sure though."

José grabbed my arm and pulled me towards the couch. "We should get started."

Tasha wasn't finished with me though. "Wait," she said. Her margarita swished dangerously close to the edge of her glass. "How are Russian Studies, Sports, and HR related? What kind of quiz was this? I think you need to meet with a professional."

"I don't know. It said something about utilizing my analytical problem solving skills, writing and...something about research abilities."

"Interesting," Amelia added, before they went back to their tacos and seemed to forget me.

José and I sat on the couch with at least twelve inches of dead space between us. He didn't hold my hand. He didn't put his arm around me.

Suddenly, a glass was in my face.

"Mocktail?" Savannah waved the cocktail dangerously close.

"No, thanks." I guided it away with my pointer finger.

"There's no alcohol, it's mostly lime juice," Tasha shouted, her voice slightly slurred.

"I'm good," I said, scooching back further on the couch and covering my stomach with a throw pillow.

"Emily, just take it." She leaned over further, dangling the liquid above me.

"Can't...allergic to limes."

"Whatev." She removed the glass from my face, and thankfully didn't pour it on my head.

It was the most miserable night of my life. I was a fool. A complete and total buffoon. It wasn't like José and I could even get any work done, Savannah there or not. Amelia and Tasha had turned up the Gypsy Kings and were singing boisterously along. And making up their own additional lyrics.

"We're the cool moms," they cackled.

"Cool mom," Amelia kind of rapped.

"Cool mom," Tasha hollered.

"Coolest moms!" Savannah encouraged them. José and I looked at each other. He mouthed, "Sorry."

But it was too late. There weren't enough sorrys to make this okay. I didn't know how I had let this happen to me, but I knew I had to take control and end it. I needed to remove myself from this situation, from José's life altogether.

Savannah returned to join us on the couch, moving to sit next to me, hovering over the seat. Changing her mind, she moved over and sat directly on José's lap and whispered something into his ear.

It was soul shattering. Like a porcupine was trying to get out of my chest, penetrating holes in my lungs and other organs. Damn my moral compass! How did it lead me so astray?

Where was my name in coat hanger lights? Was it still outside on the fence or had José disposed of any evidence of our seedy relationship? I had to stop myself from running out back and checking, or rummaging through their garbage.

I jumped up and headed to the door.

"Night," I waved.

Tasha and Amelia looked up from their huddle on the

kitchen floor and just laughed. "Cool moms," they clinked glasses, spilling one on the tile.

"Don't waste the tequila!" Amelia yelled.

She didn't. Instead Tasha slurped the margarita off the ground, and then pulled her head up and squeezed a lime into her mouth.

Classy moms. Wow, and I thought Nora was embarrassing.

José boosted Savannah off his lap, racing after me.

"I'll walk you out."

"Really, no need."

"Bye, Emily." Savannah said. "Have a good night!"

The tears started the moment I was safely outside and sprinting to my car.

José approached me while I fumbled for my keys in my bag. I finally turned to him, mid ugly cry.

"Whatever this is," I pointed to myself, then him, and then back to me, "it's over."

"Okay." He dropped his head to his chest, avoiding eye contact altogether.

"So that's it? I don't want to be a secret, so we're finished?" My voice was louder than I had wanted, and whiney.

Wasn't this when he was supposed to fight for my honor? I waited for him to beg for my forgiveness so we could get back to our happily ever after.

"You have no idea what's going on at home. My mom…" But he didn't finish his thought. He just stood there, looking at me. No sign of his smile in sight.

"My mother thinks she controls the weather. Storms and thunder and hail falling from the sky. Nothing you could tell me about your family would be weird to me. Promise."

"There's a lot of pressure on me…and…it's complicated." He seemed to struggle with what he wanted to say.

"I get it, but what are we supposed to do? Just stop living our lives? Our parents are always going to have their own stuff going on. Life is always going to be complicated. But people figure it out. If they want to be together, like *Romeo and Juliet...* but not in a dead way."

"You know...just forget it." He turned and took a few steps towards his front door.

"Forget what?" What exactly was he asking me to do? Forget him? Forget our relationship ever happened?

But he left me hanging, leaving me standing alone at my car, talking to myself. "That was totally insensitive. My mother forgot me!"

Part of me was relieved; I wouldn't have to live in turmoil any longer. He was no longer my secret boyfriend. But my irrational heart stung like I had a million paper cuts.

CHAPTER FORTY-THREE

I spent the entire night blubbering into my pillow. While my ego told me I had made the right choice to break up with José, my heart was broken. My sorrow came in waves, starting in my stomach and then rattling in my chest.

The hardest part was mourning in private. I couldn't even tell Kessia why I was so upset. She assumed it was because my mother was a mermaid and quickly lost patience with my dramatic cries.

"Stop blaming your mom for everything, Em."

Wiping my mascara stained tears onto my pillow, I snorted in an ungodly amount of snot.

"So, she's a mermaid. Get over it. Really, there are worse things that can happen," Kessia stated. Apparently she knew things I didn't.

"Like what?" I sat up.

She started listing horrendous things, proving she was right. I was being self-absorbed and maybe a tad bit ridiculous. Old Nora would have told me to suck it up and move on, but she'd make me cookies and give me a mom hug at the same time.

"Hearts break every day, Em. People live without food and clean water. Cry me a river so that I can give clean drinking water to people in need," I heard her voice in my head.

Okay, she probably wouldn't interject Justin Timberlake hits into her pep talks, but it was my psychoanalysis and I could put whatever song lyrics I wanted into them.

"I kissed José," I squeaked out.

"Sus…" Kessia whispered, shaking her head.

"A lot," I sort of bragged.

She absorbed this new sordid detail, "Anything else?"

"We had the most romantic night with flowers and the stars and…" In my mind I was back with José, in his arms, recalling that night like I had a million times before.

"Virgin?" Kessia asked, bursting my memory bubble.

"Yes! Bible."

"Then why the Tear-Fest?" As if I couldn't be sad about a boy unless we had sex. How deeply had Kessia's parents' break up affected her if she thought tears were counted by bases crossed.

"I had to break up with him." How was she not getting this? I had to break up with José to keep my integrity intact. My morals made me do it; my heart put up a good fight, but ultimately lost the inner battle.

"How do you break up with someone who has a girlfriend?" Kessia had a good point. Kind of like the sister wives' marriages aren't recognized by law, so technically they wouldn't have to get a divorce. Since José was never publicly my boyfriend was it even considered a break up?

"Exactly!" I buried my head under a pillow in frustration.

"So, you were like a mistress?" She thought out loud, "Scandalous!"

I couldn't think about it anymore. José. Savannah. The vision of her mother licking tequila off the kitchen tile floor.

What I couldn't tell Kessia, because I was having a hard time admitting it to myself, was that I was tired of feeling unworthy. Unworthy of being José 's first choice. And so unworthy that Nora didn't even want to be my mother anymore. It hurt too badly to say out loud what was on constant repeat in my thoughts and so I looked for a distraction. Something to get me out of my own head.

"I have to take my mom to swim. Wanna go?" The pool would make me feel better. And Tia's energy would be a pick-me-up.

"Hells yeah!" Kessia jumped up, always ready for the next adventure. "Don't worry," she said, and I realized that I had been worried that she'd judge me or think less of me. But she didn't. I know because she wrapped her arm around me as we headed out the door and said, "I still love you...Hussy."

AFTER INTRODUCING KESSIA TO TIA, we changed into our swim suits in the locker room.

Tia had two mermaid tails by the pool for us.

"No way! This is awesome," Kessia cheered, pulling her tail over her legs while on the bench where I usually do my homework.

"Kessia, you need to be closer to the pool," Tia instructed. "You won't be able to get in the water."

"I'm good," she gave a thumbs up. Testing the fin's weight, she lifted her legs up a few times. "It's heavy. Lots of core work."

Scooting her way off the bench, Kessia flopped onto the ground and rolled, and rolled, and rolled towards the pool like a beached dolphin. Her pink fin flapped up and down, smacking into the tile. Her extensions whirled around her face and neck into a tangled mess. Until she plopped into the water.

She began to swim, flailing about, adjusting to having her legs bound. Tia watched Kessia closely, her hands on her hips, but ready to help the floundering mermaid if needed.

"This is so hard!" Kessia shouted between breaths. "And awesome!"

It was the most ungraceful thing that I had ever seen, but Nora thought it was hilarious. I hadn't seen her laugh like that in forever, even before she had become a mermaid.

CHAPTER FORTY-FOUR

A my and I joined Gran and Fred in his yard, weeding by the front fence, goats roaming around their legs. One goat was hyper focused on Gran's fuchsia hair, nibbling at the ends. She shooed him gently away. Gran and Fred seemed to be having an old people connection.

"I like a man with a strong sense of humor."

"It's about all I've got left," Fred said with sincere honesty.

"How's your appetite for adventure?" Gran asked.

"Starving." Fred's response was giving me the feels.

"Afraid of heights?" Gran continued and I wondered if she was interviewing Fred to be her boyfriend or was thinking of hiring him to knock someone off for her. With Gran one never knew.

"I'm too old to be afraid of anything. Grim Reaper hasn't caught up with me yet. I ain't even running." Fred dabbed his head with a red bandana. I wasn't sure if it was the sun making sweat bead on his forehead or Gran's attention.

"He'll do just fine," Gran announced to Amy and I, as if Fred couldn't hear her. Or maybe he couldn't. Hearing aids and all. But I could have sworn Fred blushed somewhere under his age spots and wrinkles. It was beyond cute.

Wonderful. Cupid had come to Columbus and shot Kessia and Jack, Mom and Dad, and Gran and Fred, with his love arrows, bypassing me altogether.

Amy and I got to work cleaning out the rabbit pens, while Nora collected eggs, telling the hens what a great job they had done and ensuring them that we would not eat their children.

When Dad arrived, Amy and I were relaxing on the porch, each holding a bunny and Nora massaging a goat. "Nora, I got you something."

"It's a fish tank. Saltwater," Gran said, spoiling Dad's surprise.

If Nora couldn't be in the ocean, Dad would bring it to her. It was a sweet gesture.

"A huge tank full of colorful fish like the show Mommy's been watching? *Tanked*?" Amy asked. "I'm so excited! Nora, a tank!"

"It's not like that, Amy. Just fifty gallons," Dad said, deflated as if the fish tank was a representation of his manhood.

"Nora, is that a new ring?" Gran asked, referencing a gold-plated starfish ring where mom's wedding ring once lived.

"It is," Nora batted her mink eyelashes. "We're engaged!"

"Congratulations," Fred cheered.

"Yeah, Mommy," Amy added, examining the ring. "Such a pretty starfish."

"So, you're cheating on your wife with your wife?" Gran asked, laughing at her own joke.

"Mother…" Dad scolded.

"Ever hear of making the same mistake twice?" She leaned forward and her voice was more serious.

"Mother, Nora is the love of my life." I breathed a sigh of relief. Even if my mother had abandoned me, I didn't want dad to leave her.

"Which one? The attorney or the mermaid?" Dad was right,

sometimes Gran wasn't funny. Nora was still Nora, or a version of her. I think, at least. She was still my mom...ish.

"You're impossible," Dad retorted, clearly annoyed that Gran didn't congratulate.

So, my parents were getting married again. Apparently my father had been a lousy husband, but was an excellent pirate. At least a wedding would keep Nora here beyond Amy's recital. I guess that was a good thing, except the likelihood that the event would be pirate and mermaid themed made it less exciting. And the fact that I wouldn't have a date. But maybe my mom would know she was my mom by then and we'd be a real family again. School would be out soon and I could focus more on my case, and I'd have mom's genetic testing results any day now. I was banking on the DNA to be the indisputable proof I needed. I was running out of options.

CHAPTER FORTY-FIVE

D ad was taking Nora to the Wildlife Safari Park in Ashland because she wanted to see the land locked animals while she was here. They were taking the 1984 Ford mom had traded her car for, just in case Nora saw any more strays to bring to Fred's sanctuary.

"No elk or bison under the sea, huh?" Gran scoffed.

We went to the drive-through park two summers ago. Having been up close and personal with wolves and bears was pretty awesome. Nora loved it and she would love it again as a mermaid.

"We will be back tomorrow before noon."

"It's an hour-and-a-half away. Doesn't really warrant an overnight." I said, but was relieved to have a break from watching my mother. It was more stressful than I'd realized and I could feel my shoulders relaxing with the just the thought of them leaving together.

"We're staying in Lincoln."

So, my Pirate Father and Mermaid Mother were having a rendezvous in our State's capitol, and I was stuck at home grounded and single.

"We're getting matching anchor tattoos!" Nora shared. Wow, Bart. Subtle.

"Have a good time!" Gran scooted them out the door. Before they were even out the driveway she looked at me. "What are you waiting for? They're good as gone. Amy and I can keep ourselves busy."

Whether or not I was sneaking out was a technicality. Or a loop hole. Or as Nora would refer to it, "Subject to interpretation."

Yes, I was grounded, but Dad put Gran in charge and she was *ordering* me to go out.

"Live your life," she shouted. "Carpe Diem."

"What's that?" Amy asked.

"Seize the day...You will have no regrets, but for the times you didn't take chances." Gran kept throwing out clichés as I frantically got ready to go.

"Are these shorts too short?" I asked, checking the mirror one more time for any signs of underwear showing.

"Can anyone see your vulva?"

"No!" God, Gran was raunchy.

"You're good. Go!" She shooed me like a bug, waving her hands at me until I was out the front door. I heard the door lock behind me, not so much to keep her and Amy safely inside, but to make it clear that I was not welcomed back until I'd completed a night of debauchery. Do most people's grandparents encourage them to be wild and free?

I flip-flopped between feeling like a model and a clown with so much make-up on. The foundation I'd caked on was hot and suffocating, and my eyelashes were so heavy my eye lids were hanging at half-mast.

Kessia ran to my car as I was climbing in. I reached over and unlocked her door, trying to decide if her shorts were shorter than mine.

"You have the list?" She burst out. "Give it to me!"

I handed it over and she read it out loud while I cringed.

Each word was physically ripping my deeply imprinted childhood out through my skin.

Nora's Rules

1. No heavy make-up

She looked me over and decided I had contoured enough face paint to freak out old Nora. "Done. Check," she announced.

2. No skanky short shorts

"Done. Do I look skanky?" I was seriously second guessing shorts where my pockets were longer than the denim.

"Yes, but in a good way," she answered, sounding a bit too much like Gran for my comfort.

3. No drinking

"What about smoking or vaping?" Kessia asked as if Nora had forgotten.

"She knows I cough around smoke and get a raging headache. No desire there." Yes, Nora knew I would never smoke because I couldn't even stand being around smokers.

4. No staying out past 10 p.m. curfew

"Easy." She sped up, clearly losing interest in Nora's premermaid rules.

5. No being alone with boys i.e. bedroom, his house, etc., etc.

"Like ever?"

I shrugged. "Not really sure."

6. No riding in back of trucks

7. But before she could read lucky number seven, her voice trailed off.

"There's more?" She crumpled up the paper and tossed it on the floor of my car.

"Yeah, I ran out of time. Gran was pushing me out the door."

Kessia rubbed her cheeks one last time and faced me. "Okay, we may have to combine some of these, but we can do it! The night is ours!"

What were we going to do? The possibilities seemed limitless. My first high school party? A rave? A circus? I had no clue what Kessia had planned.

"Turn in there," she pointed to the Taco Bell parking lot.

"A bean burrito? That's hardly the rebellious night out I thought I was getting."

"The night is young, Em. Trust me." She knew I would, but I tried to hide my disappointment. Although I do love tacos.

A jacked-up truck with obnoxiously big tractor tires pulled up next to us. It looked like trouble and evoked thoughts of jumping off roofs into pools, shopping cart races through parking lots, and drag racing on an abandoned road. It even had flames painted on the side. If I were a cop, this was the truck I would pull over. For sure.

"That's Jack's new truck. Let's go," Kessia grabbed her purse and exited my car.

"That's our ride? Really? Nora would be appalled," I said to myself, locking my car and leaving it in the Taco Bell parking lot. "It's perfect."

CHAPTER FORTY-SIX

S tud Muffin Jack rolled down his window. "Your chariot awaits."

Kessia batted her eyes and giggled. Apparently, Mr. Edwards had quite the matchmaking talent. Was he aware of his English project love connections? Did he match students on purpose, or was this a subliminal talent he wasn't aware of? Maybe it was all of Shakespeare's love stories that gripped a hold on our young hearts. Whatever it was, Mr. Edwards had struck gold.

Kessia was in love.

Benny helped us climb into the monster truck cab, joining Enrique, who I considered the second hottest boy in school, right behind José. Was it possible that my love compass was off? Maybe I was supposed to be with Enrique. Maybe he would profess his undying love for me in a public forum. Or maybe I needed to get all of these Shakespeare plays out of my head.

We cranked down the street and around town, until we took a slight left into a field of nothing.

Benny held up his phone and nodded towards Enrique, "Tell your mom to stop adding me."

"I blocked your mom days ago," Enrique joked back.

After driving for a while, I noticed that Enrique's arm was around me. It was heavy and awkward, unlike the comforting touch of José. It wasn't bad, just different, so I was determined to ease into the feel of someone else.

I saw smoke in the distance and soon we were up close and personal with a bonfire and half the high school. M.O.N. was the spot to meet and everyone was off in their typical cliques and groups. Though it technically wasn't the "middle of nowhere," it was where a teenager from long ago had decided was M.O.N., and generations of teenagers had gravitated to this destination ever since like fireflies to light.

Kessia and I walked around the fire and mingled with some of the girls from P.E.

"You're so with Jack," I said, happy for her.

"Yeah, I'm going to rip his heart out, or he's going to shred mine. It won't be pretty either way."

"I'm glad you're sharing your love with someone other than Fred's goat."

"Enrique is nice to look at."

"He is."

He was really handsome. His chiseled jaw and mischievous smile sent shivers down my spine. Rumor had it he was the best kisser at school. I wondered if I was objectifying him as I stared at his perfectly plumped lips, the kind women on housewife reality shows pay a ton of money for.

"Want to go for a walk?" Enrique asked, grabbing my hand.

His hands were big, and rough, with smooth parts that had not yet calloused.

"Sure," I looked back at Kessia. She winked.

We walked away from the fire and over towards the lake. Other couples had veered off and were making out. It was like lover's lane of M.O.N. Technically, I wasn't fully alone with Enrique, but we did put enough distance between ourselves and another couple so that it wasn't awkward. It was dark enough to see the stars and water, along with the fire in the distance where some kids danced around while others just rough housed and bumped into one another.

He pulled me closer, and lifted my chin.

"So, we're doing this?" I asked, buying time and space between us.

"You want to?" he asked politely.

I appreciated his manners. Nora would be proud of his respect towards a female he was about to kiss.

"Yes."

And his lips were on mine before I finished, devouring me. It wasn't exactly aggressive, but it was passionate. Only since I didn't really know him, or have any feelings for him, it feel kind of fleshy, and wet, and mechanical.

I raised my arm up instinctively and ran my fingers through his thick hair. God, he was gorgeous. But there wasn't any tingling in my stomach. Or excitement. Or anything.

And then I got sad. Tears started in my throat and then came bursting out of my eyes. I pulled away from Enrique.

"You okay?" he asked, genuinely concerned.

Why didn't I like him? He really was a nice guy, and so incredibly good-looking. Why couldn't I turn my feelings off for José? Or transfer them to Enrique? Stupid, stupid love.

"Let's just go back."

"Okay. I get it." It was nice of him to try and understand, but I wasn't sure what he 'got.' Did he think I was upset about my mother being a mermaid? Or did he know I was still in love with José? Or did he think I just wanted to go back to the fire? We probably should have talked some more, but I didn't even know what to say.

He guided me back to the fire and we found Kessia and Jack talking to a group of kids. Jack had his arm around Kessia and they kept exchanging looks. It was incredible to see her so happy. I wiped my eyes, determined not to feel sorry for myself.

CHAPTER FORTY-SEVEN

"Who wants to knee board?" Jack asked the crowd. "Here? Where's the boat?" There didn't seem to be a dock or a boat ramp.

"He'll pull someone from his truck," Kessia informed me. "The rope is long enough to pull someone along the shore. It's dope."

Yeah, dope as in incredibly stupid.

Plenty of guys raised their hands and hollered. One girl volunteered, but her friends all giggled around her. Was everyone here nuts? Or was I just paranoid? Why did everyone think this was a good idea, but me?

"Enrique, My Main Man, you're first up!"

Some guys piled in the back of Jack's truck, while he helped Kessia into the passenger seat.

"Em, come on," she called out.

If I was going to break more of Nora's rules, I had to get on with it, so I climbed into the back of the truck and smashed myself between Benny and a football player.

Jack took off with a yank and removed the slack from a long rope. At the end of the rope was a handle, which Enrique held onto, while seated on a knee board. As the truck moved forward, Enrique glided into the shallow water and began maneuvering out further along the shore.

What was I so worried about? Everything seemed to be fine. Just a truck pulling a knee boarder down the shore. I really needed to chill out and have fun. Why did being a rebellious teenager feel so awkward for me?

"Hey Enrique, your mom's story is my junk," Benny hollered, grabbing his balls. I wished I could move away from him.

The football player I was wedged next to cheered and then spilled a beer down my back. "Sorry, my bad."

Jack sped up, and swerved around a rock, creating slack in the rope, yanking Enrique's arms. He flipped into the air and landed on his neck, his legs still strapped onto the board. It happened so fast I could have missed it if I wasn't looking.

A collective gasp escaped from everyone in the truck. Enrique whipped back around so his board was back on the ground, but he had let go of the rope. This was not good. Bodies are not made to be contorted into that position and be okay.

My gut was on fire and I knew this was really bad, like life changing bad. One of the guys was banging on the window, screaming for Jack to circle back. "He's hurt! Hurry!" Two guys jumped out of the truck in motion and raced to Enrique in the sand. Jack backed us up so that the guys could load Enrique and lay him down.

"Hold his head," someone shouted at me. I braced Enrique's shoulders as they placed him carefully into my lap. I heard the tail gate snap close.

"I'm so sorry if I'm hurting you," I told him, looking into his eyes. He was silent, starring off into space, his mouth hanging open.

"Go. Get him to the hospital!" Someone pounded on the top of the truck, and we slowly moved forward in the night.

Enrique looked like a Roman statue, masculine and perfect, but extremely breakable. One of the guys knelt next to him and held his body up. Another one held his feet. "You're going to be okay, Bro," said one.

"You got this," said another.

"I didn't mean it about your mom," Benny wept.

I stayed frozen, afraid to move, or breathe, cradling his head in my arms. I didn't know how much pain he was in, or what was happening, or if he was going to die. Twenty minutes ago, he was kissing me. His perfect lips on mine. His healthy limbs wrapped around me.

Was he going to be a quadriplegic? Or paralyzed from the waist down? Was his football career over? My lungs hurt. My arms ached, begging for a break, but I refused to give up. I didn't want to let him down.

"We're almost there," Kessia called from the front seat. "Hold on, Enrique."

Jack pulled into the emergency entrance and hospital workers quickly met us, moving us to the side and strapping Enrique onto a gurney. Kessia had called ahead so they were ready for our arrival, wheeling Enrique in past the electric opening. It shut behind him and we all watched him disappear.

Tears escaped my eyes and I worried about Enrique's fate. It didn't seem fair. Nothing was fair.

The truck started moving again as Jack maneuvered towards the visitor's parking lot. I looked in and saw him texting while driving. Yes, we were in a parking lot and only going a few miles per hour, but still. I lost it. Banging on the window.

"Stop texting and driving!"

"Woooh, Em. Calm down," Kessia said.

"I have a contract!" I screamed.

I had a contract not to text and drive, or be in the car with anyone who was texting and driving. I was breaking my contract with my mother. I was in the back of the truck; it was after 10 pm; and, I had on short shorts and make-up. I was a rule breaker and it wasn't fun, or cool, or anything to brag about.

I wanted to be a rebel and figure out who I was, but it turns out I don't want to be a rule breaker. I don't want to hurt anymore. I don't want Enrique to die. And I don't want to call my father, who is going to kill me with his bare hands. Everything was so totally messed up.

I contemplated pretending I'd lost my mind and was a mermaid. As if mom was infectious. It was basically true at this point. My entire life was being held together by glitter glue. In this moment of hell, it all suddenly made perfect sense as to why my mom would want to jump into the ocean and swim very far away.

CHAPTER FORTY-EIGHT

Nobody spoke in the waiting room. Kessia fell asleep, her head in Jack's lap, who played a game on his phone. The guys all stretched out in various positions, some were on their phones, others prayed.

A doctor came out and told Enrique's parents that Enrique was going to be okay, though they weren't sure about any extensive damage yet. He had broken his neck and would be wearing a neck stabilizing brace for at least eight weeks, and there'd be years of rehabilitation. Since we all blatantly listened, when we should have given them privacy, we collectively exhaled.

Enrique was going to be okay.

"I'm so grateful. So, so thankful," I said out loud, tears streaming from my eyes. "He's going to be okay." Enrique's mom hugged me, but no one else acknowledged my mini-celebration, so I sat back down in awkward silence.

We got picked up one-by-one from angry parents.

Bart arrived close to midnight. He looked ridiculous in his pirate costume, but no one said anything. No one cared that my father looked like he just got off his shift as a fry cook at Long

John Silver's. I followed him out to the car, and got in the passenger side, awaiting the wrath of disappointment.

"I don't believe in past lives, or future lives, but if there are any..." he started, but it wasn't angry talk, it was more reflective. And confusing.

"I'll be grounded for them all. Got it." I said, wanting him to know I did get it. I understood how stupid I had been to go out and break Nora's rules.

"No sarcasm tonight, please." He sounded like he was giving up on me, like he couldn't take one more minute of my existence.

I wasn't being sarcastic, at least I wasn't trying to be. I knew I had crossed every parental boundary line and I had accepted it the moment Enrique flipped in the air, but I couldn't find the words to let dad know what I meant.

"You know, there's a difference between rules we make as parents and state laws. You get that, right?" He asked, one hand on the steering wheel.

"Yes, Sir." It was all I could think of that wouldn't start a fight.

"I love you, Em. But I'm really mad at you," he sighed, that sigh that says I'm too tired to even care about you anymore. It hurt.

I was really mad at me too.

Once we were home, we both grabbed some water from the fridge. I lingered by him, not quite ready to go to bed. I didn't have my mom and I couldn't lose my dad too.

"She was always my barometer, you know. Her voice rings in my ear, whether she's there or not. *Do the right thing. Be truthful. Honor and justice.* Whenever I had doubts about something, I knew just by looking at her where she stood and then I'd stand there too. I blindly trusted everything she said as absolute law. And now...I'm just floundering." The words poured out of me.

"Yeah, it sucks, Em. But you're growing up and are going to have to act like it or there will be consequences. And I don't

mean here, I mean out there. In the real wor
outside with both hands, then took his water to
and plopped down into his favorite chair, stari
walls.

"I know about the genetics test," he said as
given him the last bit of energy he needed to fi
sation with me. "I'm assuming you didn't need
lab. I'm also fairly confident that you're not tryi
mother."

"It's the proof I need. She's always been a
building a case. When she sees the results, it c
attorney part in her brain that's buried so dee
dripped from my eyes landing on my shirt. "I ju:
I'm scared she's never coming back."

"I'm sorry, Emily. I know this has been hard
were wet. His fist clutched the wood end on tr
his hand red and white around the knuckles. ".
should leave the memory rebuilding to the doct
himself out of the chair and patted my bac
heading to his bedroom.

I snuck into Amy's room and climbed into he
could save her from growing up and making I
me. I wanted to save her from the kind of physic
went through, and the endless dull ache that ne
recently broken heart. I inhaled her innoc
remember a time when I didn't feel the world c
around me, before I knew about poverty and
tragedies. And mothers deciding to become mer

Realizing those carefree days were over, I sl
my own room, pulling my comforter over my h
don't ever get to go back to when Nora kept me
everything bad. The blinders were officially off
was over.

CHAPTER FORTY-NINE

y morning started like any other morning, me checking
Snapchat stories from bed. Benny had caught the
que accident on his phone and I had to relive it for a few
ing seconds. It looked so painful. If I didn't already know
as going to be okay, I'd have a heart attack.

)nce I was done with stories, I swiped into the news, and
s when I saw the daily Buzzfeed was a photo of my mother,
her mermaid glory, with the caption, "Is There a Mermaid
emic?"

Vhat?!?

screamed a horror movie scream, startling the animals next
at Fred's.

)aring myself to move forward, I chose the pic of Nora,
ing it into the article on my phone. Turns out, it was Tia's
maid Phenomenon video, and it had gone viral.

'or 2 minutes and 45 seconds, Tia's voice spoke about the
y roles of women and when it all becomes too much. I
the closed captioning, "Mermaids have long been a staple
1ythology, but what about modern times? When women
l a mental break, where can they go? One small town

woman has become a mermaid… and the trend is catching on."

Kessia came plowing into my room, jumping onto the bed.

"Holy Fishballs! Your mom's face is everywhere," she announced before sliding down to the floor beside me.

Calling Tia, I put her on speakerphone, holding the phone between us.

"Yeah, sorry Emily. It was first picked up by Hello Giggles and then Good Morning America. From there, it made the circuit in various newsfeeds like Yahoo and HuffPost. I didn't have any intention of making this video public," Tia's voice echoed through the room.

"It's not your fault," I said. "Is it?"

Tia continued, her calm voice nudging me out of my panic, "My professor uploaded it to YouTube. He didn't think anyone outside of our class would view it. But one person shared it on Facebook, and then it kind of went from there. I'm so sorry. I never planned to invade your mother's privacy."

I forced myself to take deep breaths. Kessia acted like my Lamaze coach, encouraging me to inhale.

"Emily, have you seen the whole thing?" Tia asked.

"No, not yet," I looked at Kessia; she shook her head no.

"You should," she said. "See you at the pool."

Kessia and I perched on the edge of my bed and started the video from the beginning. Mid-way I found out why she wanted me to view it all. There I was. Dripping wet in my clothes saying what a mermaid means to me, "Mother."

I had one word in a viral video and it was absolutely mortifying.

"Kessia, do you see how forever this is?"

"People will totally forget about it in five minutes or less." She got up and started rummaging through my closet.

"But what about right this moment?" I screeched.

"No one cares, Emily. It's fun for like a second and then we all move on with our day," she pulled a skirt from the far end of the closet. "And why is this beauty hiding back here?" She slipped it on over her pajamas and then yanked the pajamas off from underneath it.

"I have my forever slogan now, and it's not even about me. It's an extension of my mother," slumping back onto my bed, I piled pillows around me like a cocoon. "That looks good on you," I referenced the skirt I had forgotten about.

"What do you mean?" She turned in front of my long mirror on the back of my bedroom door.

"I've spend my entire existence trying to keep myself un-identifiable, not in any clique, no distinct markings, no labels, and now I will be known as 'The Mermaid's Daughter,'" I groaned and placed the final pillow over my head, hoping I could disappear and return to the world as a butterfly in a few short days.

"I'm so making a t-shirt of that," she exclaimed.

"What?!?" To match the skirt? Kessia always went off on tangents, but I wasn't following. Why would she be making a t-shirt? So much for my metamorphosis. I threw off the pillows as she brought my laptop to my bed.

"People love mermaids. It's big business. You gotta jump when the trends hit." She brought up her web store on my computer. "I started it over a month ago when your mom caught her virus or whatever. Just kind of messing with some ideas, but it caught on."

I scanned the page; she was selling t-shirts, mugs, and pajama sets.

One design read *Instant Mermaid: Just Add Salt Water* and had a picture of an adorable mermaid inside a tea cup. Another showed a sassy mermaid seated sideways on the back of a motorcycle with the word *Salty* underneath.

"Kessia, my mother is mad sick and you're making t-shirts?!?" I exclaimed while still pushing the down arrow key to scroll through her page.

"Yes. Want one?" She yanked her pajama pants back on and took off my skirt we both knew she was taking.

"No...and people think you're the lazy one." She was actually a business savant disguised as a teenager in a petite bow.

"I identify as lackadaisical. It's less permanent," Kessia went back to shopping, trying on my shoes.

"How did you not tell me about this, Kes?"

"Really? Miss I'm secretly dating José for weeks without telling my best friend, I guess that's where our friendship is headed as we mature into adults. Secrets, lies and deception... and profits. Can I borrow these flats?"

Did anyone else have a best friend who could squeeze money from any situation? I had to face the facts, all signs were pointing to Kessia as my future boss. I just hoped she'd pay well and provide a decent healthcare package.

CHAPTER FIFTY

We were on self-imposed house arrest since Tia's video had gone viral and a storm was coming, possibly a tornado. Since the media didn't know who mom was, Tia was fending off interviews, and the rest of us were just staying out of sight and waiting for the storm to pass. Some of the locals in Columbus knew about mom being the viral mermaid, but thankfully, everyone was respecting her privacy.

Nora painted glitter onto plates and bowls at the dining room table, while Gran French braided Amy's hair.

"Nora, don't do that! You're ruining my mother's wedding China!" I said before catching myself. It was pointless to argue about my old mother to my mermaid mother.

"She's fine," Gran said. "And really likes sparkles."

"Got it." I said, checking the sky again.

It was getting darker and gloomier, like my mood. I'd always loved storms as a kid, but now it just seemed to magnify the pending doom I felt. José wasn't even talking to me, not that I wanted him to. But I did.

"She's arrived," Janet entered, carrying an overnight bag. "Hail the size of golf balls just blocks away."

"Turn on the news," Gran commanded. "We can track it."

"Mom doesn't like the news on. It makes her sad," Amy worked on her own glitter art at the table.

"We can make an exception," I said to Amy, "It's kind of an emergency."

I flipped to our local channel and saw that our mayor was being interviewed. The weather report scrolled across the bottom of the screen. I tried to read it as it quickly flashed by.

"Turn it up," Janet commanded.

"Bowfin, catfish, silverside," the Mayor of Columbus was listing the fish of Nebraska. "Perch, bass.

The woman interviewing him seemed annoyed. "Yes, but what about this mermaid we've been seeing so much of online?"

The Mayor scratched his head and appeared to be thinking. "No, we don't have mermaid's in Columbus. We do have trout, pike…"

Janet muted the T.V. "I guess we'll just read the weather report."

Nora started to cry. And squeak.

"Okay, no news at all. I'll turn it off!" I marched directly to the TV and turned it off manually.

"It's just…I'm so sorry," Nora put her paint brush down, trying to compose herself.

Amy moved her chair closer to mom to console her, "It's okay, Mom. Let's do our art. Glitter makes you happy."

"It's all my fault," Nora whimpered.

Janet rushed over, guiding Nora from the dining room chair to the couch so she could lay down.

"I can't help it; you know…the storm." Nora pulled the blanket Janet gave her up around her, all the way up to her chin. She looked pale and sickly and I feared her physical health was getting as bad as her memory.

Janet gently adjusted a pillow, "Are you fearful of storms, Nora?"

"No! It's my fault. I caused it." She sat up and then fell back into the couch.

"Nebraska has had storms for like forever. Since time began," I said, "This happens every single summer." I was trying to make her feel better, but it came out condescending. Why couldn't I stop sounding like a jerk?

"This one is all me. It's my sadness. I can't control it any longer," she sat up, finding her strength. "I'm warning you guys. Please take caution. Until I return to the Pacific Ocean…there will be more."

"More storms, Mommy?" Amy asked, kneeling beside her like the devoted daughter she was.

"Yes, the longer I'm away from home the more my emotions get the best of me. I can't help but create rough waters." Nora wrapped an arm around Amy protectively. "I always seem to create rough waters when I'm upset. One time…"

"Oh, hold on, I'll get snacks." Gran flew into the kitchen and pulled out the popcorn maker. She loved when Nora went off on her made up ocean adventures. Gran said it was like witnessing an audio book and an 'absolutely fascinating' glimpse into mom's mind.

"Emily," Nora called out and I went to her as if the couch was a hospital bed. Amy moved away so that I could get closer.

"Yes?" I asked, wondering if she was going to ask me to restrain her until the storm passed. Maybe if she drank a refreshing beverage I could convince her that the storm inside her was snuffed out, saving all of Nebraska. I leaned in close so she could whisper in my ear.

"I'm dying on land. When are you taking me?" Though she was barely audible, I knew what she was asking. I backed away, unsure what to do.

"We had a deal," she cried out, looking helpless.

"What deal, Mommy?" Amy asked, wedging herself between us and handing Nora a cup of tea. "I want to hear all about the tides. Can you tell me about some of your adventures?"

As Nora delved into stories about causing tidal waves and ship wrecks, I retreated into my bedroom. We had made a deal and I had no intention of keeping. Once again, I was going against my entire belief system. And to make things worse, Nora thought I was going to save her and I couldn't even save myself.

I checked every social media account on my phone for any signs of José. He hadn't posted, commented or liked anything in days. Giving up, I turned on my lap top, and heard a knock at my door. Or maybe it was the hail hitting the roof.

Another knock.

"Come in," I shouted as Janet entered.

"I should go out and check the animals," I started, sure that she was coming to get me to do just that. Janet probably thought I was being lazy for hiding in my room and escaping from my mom's mermaid testimony.

"They're not your responsibility," Janet said. "You do not have to save the animals."

"...but the storm." The animals would be wet and cold and smelly. Or maybe my mom had told Janet about our deal. Was I going to get a lecture on lying to my mother even if she was slightly incoherent?

"You're just like your mom. Always taking care of everyone else. Everything else. You assumed that you have to take care of them, but Fred can hire some high school boys to help out." Janet looked out the window, accessing the animal situation at Fred's, "You can't do it all by yourself, Emily."

Was she talking about my mother or the animals? Or both?

"But someone has to feed them. And make sure Fred doesn't let the chickens poop all over his house. He'll die!" In all seriousness, it was terrifying to imagine Fred lying on the floor, surrounded by bird droppings as he gasped for breath.

Janet sat at my desk. "And just like your mother, sometimes

you have to ask for help." She spun around on the chair to face me.

Slow, leaky tears formed in my eyes and squished out no matter how hard I tried to hold them back. Janet would most likely think I was weak for crying. She'd seen horrendous cases of abuse from people who probably never shed a tear. Or maybe she had cried so much she was all dried up. Do we ever run out of tears?

"I'm pretty good at this whole college prep stuff. Do it all day long. Financial aid and all," she picked up the career book I had checked out from the library and flipped through it.

"Really?" Was Janet offering to help me?

"I've been known to crawl inside a teenager's head and yank out their wildest dreams...and well, what they're good at." She stopped on a page and read it out loud, "Which college is your right fit?"

"I always thought my mom would help me with all this. I don't know what I want to do and I'm supposed to be picking classes and schools and everything. It's just so much...stuff." I threw my hands up and shrugged. "I don't know what to do or what I want to do."

"Would you like my help?" she offered.

I just hugged her. There were no words for the relief that pulsed through my body; wiping away weeks of fear and intimidation. For the first time since my mom had turned into a water sprite, I didn't feel so alone. Janet asked questions and gave me suggestions, talking me through what I would be good at and the career options different degrees presented. She didn't rush me or make me feel stupid either. In fact, she did dig into my brain, finding all kinds of artifacts and pretty things hidden away in there.

We were interrupted by Fred and Dad, who needed help sheltering some of the animals from the storm, but Kessia and Jack were already hard at work when we arrived. Janet was right. The animals were not just my responsibility. We had all stepped up. There we were, being pelted by hail, covering the rabbit and pig pens with wood, while Nora watched silently at the window.

"I'm sorry," she mouthed to Dad when he waved up at her, still taking ownership of the massive thunder pounding through the sky. Nora the Mermaid honestly believed that she was more powerful than Mother Nature.

CHAPTER FIFTY-ONE

Amy laid out sets of matching pajamas on the couch. They had stripes of Christmas trees and candy canes on the pants and huge reindeer faces on the tops, each with a sparkling red nose. "Here, Daddy, this is your size. Em, that's yours."

"Why are we planning for Christmas in May?" I asked, "On Mother's day?"

"It's tradition." Amy put her hands on her hips. "Remember." It wasn't a question; it was a command from my six-year old sister. She wanted me to conjure up some memory of something that didn't exist.

Every Mother's Day for as long as I could remember we delivered new sets of pajamas to women's shelters, homeless shelters, and men's shelters, though there wasn't many of those. Nora was always careful not to gender discriminate for those in need.

"Amy let me know about the pajama tradition," Nora exclaimed, wearing her mermaid crown with the festive pajamas. "It's so fun. Matching family pajamas! I love Mother's Day!"

Dad swooped up his pajamas and went to put them on. He gave me a look and said, "Family tradition, Em. Put 'em on."

As much as I was glad Dad was trying with mom and had seemed to save their marriage, I didn't see why I had to play along. "But why are they Christmas pajamas?"

"You try to find matching sets!" Amy shouted. "It's my recital and mom's day. Put them on!"

My sister's freak out reminded me that Nora wasn't allowed to wear her mermaid attire to the recital. Amy's dance teacher had made that very clear, so poor Amy was just trying to get Nora into anything else. There was little chance we could get that mermaid crown off her, but I guess holiday pajamas are a little less distracting. A tiny bit.

"Oh, right. Tradition." I mumbled as I took my set into my bedroom.

In case I wasn't completely humiliated by the fact that my immediate family was dressed for the holiday season, Amy had ordered pajamas for Gran and Fred as well. We caravanned to the auditorium and arrived looking like we were scheduled to be a part of a holiday parade. I tried not to make eye contact with anyone watching as we made our way into the recital.

"Program." A wide-eyed ballerina handed me a pamphlet.

"Thanks."

She snorted between giggles, turning to watch us enter the rows of seats.

I knew by now that taking Nora anywhere meant I needed to check my exit route. I had to have a plan in the event that she had a meltdown. How would I get her out of the building as quickly as possible? The auditorium was quickly filling up, so getting a number of seats together became less likely.

"Over here!" A woman called to us, dressed entirely like a mermaid. She looked like a bad version of well, Nora. "Nora, I saved you and your family seats!"

Great. We were in the mermaid section. Astounding.

"I'm so inspired by Nora," the woman told us as we shuffled

into our row. "She's really taught me to listen to my inner-mermaid."

"Seriously?" I couldn't help myself. The one day I thought we were getting a reprieve.

"You should be proud of your mother," the woman glared at me.

Awesome. It's always nice to be shamed in public by someone who doesn't know me at all. Thanks for judging me, Lady. But fortunately Nora raised Amy and I to value our own feelings. I'm allowed to be upset my mom has forgotten me, thank you very much.

"I've never felt more free." She beamed again at Nora and my dad.

"That's great," Dad smiled at her, holding mom's hand.

"Careful," Gran tapped me with her elbow. "It's contagious. There's another one headed this way."

So much for the new "no mermaid" rule at dance class. I rolled me eyes as Gran and Fred scooted down through the seats to make room for another mermaid who joined us.

"Hi, Nora. Our daughters are in dance together. I've always wanted to just be myself too," she adjusted her mermaid crown. It was slightly better than Nora's, with strands of pearls hanging delicately around her face, gold shells sparkling under the lights. "I'm switching careers. I'm training to be a professional mermaid this summer in Cancun."

"Being a professional is hard work," Nora commented. "You have to be able to free dive in salt water, which is harder for human eyes, and not be distracted by all kinds of fish. Usually grouper, barracuda, eels. I still don't trust eels since our last encounter."

Nora winked at my dad and then squeezed his hand, as if they actually had an encounter with eels. Really, it was an endless sea of nonsense. I huffed in my seat, crossing my arms over my scratchy reindeer nose.

Why was everyone appeasing her? It was as if the entire

population had a town hall and had voted to act like dressing like a mermaid was not only normal, but to be emulated. How had I missed this meeting?

"Move over one," Kessia commanded. "And put on the antlers."

"Better?" I asked, a scowl on my face, antlers on my head like the rest of my family, sans Nora in the crown.

"Nobody likes a grouchy reindeer." Kessia scooched in between Gran and I. "We're here for Amy. And Nora."

"Yeah, we'll you're not dressed as Rudolph."

"No one cares." Kessia sighed, digging out a bag of gummies from her purse. "Breakfast?"

The lights dimmed and we could hear stomping and bumping on the stage behind the curtain. It was time for Amy and the dancer to do their thing. I sent Amy some positive energy and luck, knowing how nervous she gets before performing.

"Moms, this day is for you." Crackled through the speakers. "All the moms here, the sisters, the aunts, the grandmas, the friends, the fosters and the step-moms. The moms we have lost and the moms who have lost. The women, the men, who step up for the children. The teachers, the therapists, and anyone who nurtures. We appreciate you. And a special thank you to the moms who pay for dance."

The music blasted and the curtains began to rise, revealing a group of six-year-old tap dancers. Amy included. Her sequins vest sparkled almost as bright as her smile. As a dance teacher over-exaggerated their steps on the side, the girls and two boys clomped and shuffled on the stage.

Nora smiled brightly, watching Amy with enthusiasm. Standing and clapping as the number finished and the dancer took their bows. Back in her seat, Nora's energy changed. I could feel her shaking.

"Nora, what is it?" I asked.

"I just…I wish I could be your mom." She said and I saw tears dripping down her cheeks.

"It's okay, really. You were the best mom for sixteen years of my life. It's okay, Nora." I tried to comfort her, but she just sobbed harder.

"Let's go, Nora." Dad said, standing.

"I'll take her," Gran offered, leading Nora through the seats as the audience turned to let them through. "You stay. Amy needs you here."

Fred obediently followed Gran and Nora out to the isle.

"Should I go, Dad?" I asked, feeling torn between taking care of mom and being there for my sister.

"No. Gran's got her. And Fred. It's okay." He said, but I wasn't sure he even believed himself.

Call me if you need anything, Dad texted Gran as she walked out, her arm around Nora. Fred right behind them.

"They'll be okay, Em." He said again, and that time I really didn't believe him. Nora was getting worse. No matter how much dad didn't want to face reality, I could tell. The ocean was calling and there wasn't anything or anyone that could keep Nora the Mermaid away.

CHAPTER FIFTY-TWO

Gran had called Dad an hour after they left, after Amy had two costume changes and performances, and we were watching the recitals closing number. Nora had almost drowned.

The way Fred and Gran explained it was Nora had wanted to be near the water, even if it wasn't the ocean. So they had taken her to the Loup. Before Gran and Fred could even get their seatbelts off, Nora bolted from the car and ran into the river. She was swooped into the current and took off downstream. Although Fred valiantly tried to save her, he ultimately just hurt himself on the rocks and cracked a rib. Gran called the police, who sent a rescue team immediately.

Nora was pulled from the Loup River by two fishermen and then a helicoptor took her to the hospital. We saw a clip on the news. They kept playing it over and over, each adding commentary and facts. The other people in the hospital waiting room looked at the TV and then back to Dad, Amy and I, still wearing our holiday pajamas.

"Happy Mother's Day to me." I said to myself.

"Emily, you know what this means. Right?" Dad said. "They're going to lock her up."

Amy cried into my dad's chest, "I don't want to lose Mommy."

"She's a danger to herself, Sweetie." Dad said, not able to avoid the truth any longer. "She could get hurt."

They did keep Nora under supervision for an entire week.

The house felt cold and empty and strangely quiet. Dad and I took turns helping Fred with the animals and driving Amy around, but we were all mostly silent. No one knew what to say. Our mother was officially gone and all of our hearts were broken.

And then they brought her back.

Nora flounced into the house as if she had just run to the store and had returned. As if nothing had happened. As if she hadn't almost drowned.

"Why were you in the river?" Amy asked, "You know there's no salt in there."

"I guess, I just thought it would lead to the ocean," she admitted.

I was glad she was back, even with the stupid mermaid crown. It felt like I could breath again, but I couldn't. Not when I didn't know what was going to happen next.

There was another storm coming. The grey skys swirled above us and the thunder pounded and crackled in the air.

"Sorry," Nora said as she watched the rain fall through the window. "I cant stop it."

And I knew she couldn't. For the first time, I finally really understood that Nora wasn't faking this. That my mother I had known was gone, and I'd have to hold on tightly to this part of her that was left behind.

CHAPTER FIFTY-THREE

The last few days of school were long and tedious. I dragged myself through the halls like a zombie who had lost its appetite for flesh. Even though my family was in a constant state of emergency, I still had to go through the motions of getting an education. I wondered how many other kids at my school had nightmares going on at home. Everyone just looked bored, but maybe that's how they coped just like me.

Kessia gave me a t-shirt that read, "The Mermaid's Daughter." The design had a mermaid tail, which began on the front of the shirt and wrapped around with the fin on the back.

"On the house."

"Thanks a lot," I said, pulling it on over my tank. It was actually quite cute and fit great. Since we weren't lugging backpacks, I could show it off.

"I sold out of these puppies in less than 24 hours," Kessia boasted. She wasn't one to downplay her efforts or pretend to be coy.

"Glad you're making money off my predicament," I said and meant it.

"You're paying for my college." She stated as we slipped into our final English class of the year, she continued, "And my Kyshadow."

Mr. Edwards passed our graded projects out, and I didn't' even have an inner-party when I saw the A written in red and a note, "You put a lot of thought into this. Superb."

José wouldn't care about our A, except for the bump in his already perfect GPA. Though he earned his half of the grade, it wasn't a science or math college prep course, so he deemed it unimportant. Apparently, I was unimportant as well. I refused to turn and make eye contact with him. Not that he wanted to make eye contact with me; I just didn't want to even give him the opportunity.

The rumor was he was seeing Mandy Stephens secretly. Well, I wasn't a secret, so I sort of had my pride intact, just not my heart. I still didn't understand how I had become the villain in our short-lived relationship. Savannah and Ronnie Espinoza made their coupledom debut, holding hands and making out by the cafeteria. She stopped me as I strolled into my last history class.

"I tried to tell you." She smirked, her lips taking a short vacation from Ronnie's.

"I'm allergic to coffees…and limes."

"José really liked you. But, oh well, your loss," she hovered by me like a gnat that was too big for me to swat away. I didn't get the guy, so why was she still determined to make my life more miserable?

"He's with Mandy now. It's been three days and he's already with someone new. He obviously didn't like me that much." My annoyance and pain mix were boosting my courage.

The un-rattleable Savannah looked at me calmly, like I didn't understand social cues and she had to be really patient with me.

"Three days is an eternity," and she walked off with Ronnie, hand-in-hand.

Maybe she was right. A lot could happen in three days. A lot could happen at any moment. Look at Nora. She forgot everything in an instant.

"It's the mermaid's daughter," Benny heckled as I entered history.

"Yep." That's me. And you're a schmuck, Benny.

"So, your part fish? Ha." He looked around, making sure others acknowledged his obvious need for attention.

"Uh-huh." I kept my eyes low, wishing he'd be eaten by a giant mosquito.

"Which parts?" He high-fived one of the guys sitting next to him.

Mr. Hamm placed his hairy gorilla-sized hand onto Benny's shoulder and silenced him.

"Benny, let me inform you about the history of mermaids. You see, there are documented accounts dating back centuries, that these beautiful creatures are able to lure men to their death." Mr. Hamm removed his hairy appendage from Benny's shoulder and moved towards his desk. "I suggest you leave Emily alone and mind your own business."

Hair sprouted out of Mr. Hamm's t-shirt collar and I was glad teachers had a dress code every other day of the school year. It was a bit too much fur on display.

"Now, let's just get through these last, torturous, forty-five minutes of babysitting, so that we can all go and enjoy our summer. Shall we?"

The class kind of nodded, not sure what to do with that. He sat down in his swivel chair, putting his feet up on his desk. More hair sprung up around his last day of school flip-flops.

"Do whatever you want. Sign yearbooks. Check your Instagram. I don't care. I'm done caring." He put his head back and took a nap until the bell rung.

CHAPTER FIFTY-FOUR

Not wanting to deal or be social any longer, I pretended to go to bed early. But by 9 p.m., I was starving. I snuck into the hallway to see if I had a clear path to the kitchen, but Dad and Gran were deep in conversation.

My stomach was growling, so I decided to wait them out. And eavesdrop. Gran was mid-preach.

"Hate to break it to you, but this is all pretty normal stuff. Emily is a teenager, and Nora always worked too hard. You can't save a planet spinning through space."

"So, don't try? Don't do anything for others?" Dad asked.

"As my friends become extinct, I've learned you have to do what makes your heart sing. Nothing else matters. But you can't help anyone else, if you're not taking time for yourself. You have to live your own life too."

Amy saw me from her room. She crawled into the hallway and snuggled up next to me. We starred at each other in sister-hood silence as Dad poured his heart out.

"If she was so unhappy that she'd rather be a mermaid, I must have been a pretty awful husband."

Gran grabbed his hand. Amy pushed her body closer

against mine and I wrapped my arms around her. I could feel her tears dropping onto my arm.

"I was resentful of the time she gave to others. Selfish. I just wanted her to myself...And she did give me time. She tried to have dates and do special things for me. I was just, I don't know...unhappy myself, maybe."

"Life never turns out how we think it will," Gran said. "It's hard for everyone, ya know."

"I'm just trying to make it up to her. Maybe she'll want to come back to the family. Be my wife again. For real."

"Man up, Bart. Or pirate up. Whatever she needs right now."

"I just want her back."

He passed Gran a file. One of mom's work files.

Instinctively, I knew this was confidential territory. Mom never let anyone look at her files. They were top-secret.

I wondered if I could protect Amy from what we might hear. I didn't want it to traumatize her. But I couldn't move. I had to know what Dad was sharing with Gran though every cell in my body knew it may destroy me. That file, sitting there unopened, had the ability to spark a fear and survivor's guilt in me, knowing I was safely on the sidelines, and knowing there was horror and pain on the pages within.

"I went through her files," Dad started.

"That's breaking a few laws."

"There was one. A little girl," he swallowed and couldn't continue.

Gran passed the file back, unopened. "She'll come back to you."

Dad wiped his tears away. Nodding.

"Although I kind of like her better this way," Gran smiled lovingly at him. She took the remote and flipped through the channels. "We need something funny."

Picking a comedy movie, they stayed there. There wasn't any laughing, but the mood was slightly lifted. Amy fell asleep on the floor next to me, so I picked her up and tucked her into her bed.

An hour later, Gran almost caught me as she went into the guest bedroom, but I hid behind Amy's door until she passed. I snuck back into the hallway, obsessed with finding out what was in that folder and what was behind Dad's cryptic comment.

Dad watched another movie. My eyes were drooping, my dreams tempting me, but I held on, using my phone as my lifeline to the outside. Reading as many articles as I could and deleting all of my photos on Instagram. I just didn't want to be seen by anyone right now.

At around 3 a.m., Dad went in and out of consciousness, while an infomercial played on TV. At 4 a.m., he finally retreated into his bedroom, leaving the folder exactly where Gran had left it.

CHAPTER FIFTY-FIVE

This was what I had waited for. The answer. A front row ticket into Nora's breakdown catalyst. The one case that had pushed my mother's cognitive limits over the edge, with no return in sight.

I held the file in my hand, the one with the lipstick stain on it. The one Nora had in her hands when we were in the car accident.

My instincts were on fire, begging me to abort my mission, but I irrevocably pressed forward, opening the sacred file.

There was a picture of a little girl, her red hair all sunshiny, her smile vibrant, and a mermaid on the front of her shirt. She was beyond adorable at probably four-years-old.

And then I read the report, and I lost part of my innocence and a huge portion of my heart forever.

CHAPTER FIFTY-SIX

At 5 a.m. I dumped my backpack, leaving pencils and school supplies and wrinkled papers sprawled on the floor. Being as stealth as possible, I packed underwear, a swim suit, and enough clothes for a few days. My phone charger, a Costco pack of toothbrushes and toothpaste, a hairbrush, and lip gloss went in next.

I collected clothing for Amy and mermaid attire for Nora from the laundry room, and some towels just in case. Not wanting to wake Gran, I lubed the front door hinges with WD-40 and then took my stash to the car.

Once finished loading the car, I gently nudged Amy awake.

"What's going on?" she asked, still groggy.

"Shhhhhh. I'll explain later. Be ready to depart in five."

She jumped up and scrambled for clothes, as if we had practiced this fire drill before. I guess the new not-normal had kept her on her toes, and she met me in the hallway in under a minute.

"I'm getting mom," I whispered.

She nodded, holding her stuffed pelican.

"Nora," I nudged Mom awake.

"It's time?" she asked, hopeful.

"Yes." I was fulfilling my promise to her. Finally.

She followed Amy out, waiting as I locked the door.

"You'll send the fish, right?"

Here I was keeping my part of our deal and Nora was worried about leaving fish behind. Did she think I would Fed Ex them to the Pacific Ocean?

"Yes. I'll send them." Considering I never thought I'd be taking her to the Pacific Ocean, at this point anything was possible. Maybe I would send the fish. Life was completely and totally unpredictable and I couldn't see a day ahead. I was just moving forward by taking one step and then another.

"I'd hate for them to remain in captivity." I wanted to hug her. Nora was still thinking of others, still wanting to do what was right, even for the fish.We were on the I-80 in minutes, all three of us marveling at the sunrise. After stopping for coffee and donuts, we drove another three hours before Dad blew up our phones.

Nora answered hers first, "Bart! It's so good to hear your voice."

She listened to Dad. I chewed my lip, wondering how mad he'd be when he realized what I was up to. Wondering how quickly he'd take my car keys away.

"Emily's taking me home!" There it was, mom had told him our plan.

She listened again.

"No, my home. The Pacific Ocean." I hoped Dad's heart was healthy and not on the verge of an explosion.

They chatted a little while longer, and then she said to me, "You are to call him immediately! But not while you're driving. Bart said."

She smiled, oblivious to the amount of trouble I was in. So much that I wasn't sure if it was possible to even be in any more trouble. I was basically flushing my junior, and possibly my senior year, down the toilet. I'd be the only 17-year-old without a cell phone. Or a car. Or a life.

We all decided to stop for lunch in North Platte, so I Face-Timed Dad outside the diner. He was mid-scream at me when we connected, "of your mind, young lady."

"Dad, I owe it to mom. I have to make this right." I watched through the window, Amy and Nora ordering at the table, talking animatedly to a waitress. Oh to be young and a mermaid, free from all responsibility.

"Emily, your mother is very ill right now. She needs to be home." Dad lectured me. Me! The one who had been taking care of her since her accident.

"She wants to be in the Pacific Ocean, Dad. She deserves to go." I vowed to stand by my mom and her wishes, however odd they may seem. I had to.

"Emily!" Dad shouted, as if yelling would change my mind.

Gran popped her head into the camera's view, "Go through Utah, Darling. It's glorious."

"Mother!" Poor Bart, he was on an island of obstinate females.

"What? It is. The mountains are breathtaking. Even better if you're on the back of a motorcycle." Gran raised her eyebrows up and down and pulled the phone closer. I could see up her nose. It wasn't attractive.

"You're not helping," He scolded her. Grabbing the phone back, "Emily, bring your mother back this instant. Turn around now!"

"I have to do this." I twisted around, checking on Amy and Nora through the window. They were obliviously content.

Dad exhaled a tornado.

"Really, Dad, I want to make it right. I've never done anything for Mom and she's done so much for everybody. She wants to be in the ocean. The Pacific, to be exact, and I can take her there." I built my case.

Dad continued to exhale massive amounts of wind, until he

spoke, "You've made good time so far. I've been tracking your phones."

"Yeah," was he coming around? Or was I a dead teenager?

"Call me at every stop." He caved.

I danced around in a circle. Amy and Nora saw me from their table and danced along with me, without knowing why. Just because.

"Stop celebrating. You're still in trouble, Young Lady," Dad said, but I could tell the hostility had left his body. We said goodbye and I put my phone into my pocket, salivating as the food arrived at Nora and Amy's table.

Exhaustion hit me after an enormous burger and fries, so I laid down in the back of the car with a pillow over my head.

"I just need to sleep for a little bit," I told them. "Then we'll be back on the road."

I vaguely remember Nora wishing me sweet dreams, and then I was out.

WHEN I AWOKE, my face was stuck to the vinyl seat, a seam print across my cheek. My hair was knotted into a nest, but I'd had the sleep of a lifetime. Stretching, I realized the hum of the motor was purring. Flying upright, total hysteria hit. Nora was driving.

"I've been driving Fred around for weeks, Emily. Calm down." Nora checked the rear view mirror with ease.

"OMG. You can hardly use your legs, except swimming," I shouted, still not completely processing that Nora was behind the wheel.

"Fred's basically blind, you know," she smirked. Nora was smirking at me in the mirror, both hands on the wheel, and speeding down the highway. Why had I been her Uber for the past six weeks?

Amy just laughed, enjoying being the radio DJ and co-pilot.

"We're staying the night in Denver," Nora's voice sounded different. More confident. More like mom. The mermaid was taking charge.

"Slumber party!" Amy cheered.

Just because we were returning my mermaid mother to the Pacific Ocean didn't mean we couldn't have some fun along the way. And so I embraced the road trip and decided to go on my own mental vacation.

"Let's stay somewhere with a pool," Nora said.

"And watch movies!" Amy added.

They were right. We were staying in Denver and we should have the time of our lives before Nora left us.

"And room service!" I contributed. There was no way I was letting them be mermaid BFFs without me, and I had never had room service, so that seemed really, really cool.

We checked into the Hilban Hotel and ordered a ridiculous amount of food to be delivered to our room. We gorged on salads for Nora, and steaks with veggies for Amy and I. Our in-room movie selection was off the charts with the brand new Selena Gomez hit available. We snuggled in the bed together, each of us in a pair of mom's mermaid leggings, just sharing positive neurons, which reminded me to text Tia and let her know Nora wouldn't be at swim.

Thanks Emily. Let's hit a support group meeting when you're back. I'll join you! Tia texted back. She had given me the brochures, but I hadn't followed up. Maybe I would go with Tia when we got home.

"Let's go swimming!" I suggested and both Nora and Amy were game.

The hotel pool was enormous and inviting. We swam around, using our legs, and splashed each other as the sun started to fall lower in the sky. Colorado had mountains unlike the flats of Nebraska. I tried to soak up the different textures and altitude change. Even the air felt different.

Nora and I climbed out and lied down on two lounge chairs, watching Amy with her endless energy in the pool.

"What are you going to miss most about being human?" I asked.

"You guys the most," Nora responded without thinking. It was immediate and from the heart. She had referred to Amy and me. Maybe even in her mermaidum the motherly connection was there.

"Bart the pirate, of course. But he'll visit," she said, clearly thinking about her answer more now.

I nodded. Sure, he would. I pictured dad dressed in his pirate costume and scuba gear.

"Legs! Walking is pretty cool. And orgasms." I sort of wished she would have stopped before saying that last bit.

"Don't need to know that, Nora." Maybe this is what it felt like when your mom became your friend, when you grew up and things became different. There is still the love between you, but the relationship evolves.

"But not pooping. I won't miss that," Nora joked. I was going to miss this new, more playful Nora.

"Yeah, I wouldn't either," I chuckled.

We witnessed the most breathtaking sunset with the most brilliant colors across the sky. It was definitely a screen saver moment. Amy got out of the pool and cuddled into mom's towel.

"Sunsets," Nora sighed. "I'll miss sunsets."

CHAPTER FIFTY-SEVEN

The silky, luxurious sheets were divine, and I had slept like a goddess. Amy and Nora had shared a bed, so I had stretched out and hogged the covers all by myself. I had definitely drawn the big straw. But the more I stirred; I realized that I was in an empty hotel room.

Nora and Amy were gone, and so were my car keys.

"Noooooooo!" I yelled, scooping up my backpack and running to the elevator. "Come on, come on." I pushed the button relentlessly, before darting down the emergency stairs. Four flights later I swooshed into the hotel lobby in my pajamas. I scanned everywhere for a sign of my sister and mother, who was not the easiest person to hide.

"Have you seen a women dressed as a mermaid?" I asked the front desk.

"Yes! Just a minute ago," the clerk gloated at her co-worker. "It's the mermaid mom, from Good Morning America. I told you."

Sprinting out the front, I caught up to my posse as the valet brought my car around. I bent over from exhaustion, trying to speak.

"Amy...why?" My voice sounded like I'd crossed the desert without water.

Nora climbed into the car, tipping the valet and thanking him profusely for watching over our car all night as if he'd slept in front of it protecting it from possible vandals.

"You want to just dump her off!" Amy exclaimed.

"No, I don't."

"Yes, you do. You always complain about her!" She had her hands on her hips and I was pretty sure she was ready to have a fist fight if necessary.

"Not true." It was so true.

"I want to keep her," Amy's voice broke, a crack in her bravado.

"Amy," I was finally able to breathe upright. "Amy, I want to keep her too." She looked at me like I was a big, fat liar. Her arms folded over her chest letting me know she would not be easily manipulated like our mermaid mother.

"Honest, I swear. I'm trying to help her. She *wants* to be in the ocean. She needs to go there," I plead my case. "Don't you want her to be happy?"

"I want her home."

"Me too."

It wasn't a lie. I did want her to come home with us, but as Nora our mother.

"Ladies, I need you to either step out of the driveway, or get into the vehicle," the valet pushed us slightly towards the car and out of the way. I jumped into the car, thankful I wasn't stranded. Amy climbed into the back with Nora.

"To the Pacific Ocean," I stated.

"Hooray!" Nora clapped from the back seat.

I looked in the rear view mirror at Amy, who nodded at me in confirmation. She wasn't going to fight me on it anymore for the moment. We were still sisters, and I was relieved that our bond was still intact.

"I'm starving," Amy tapped my shoulder.

Yeah, we left without our free Continental breakfast, I wanted to say, but chose not to. I didn't want to set Amy off two minutes after making up.

"Okay. What would you like?" I asked, in spite of not knowing where any restaurants were since we left Columbus.

She pointed, "There's a Starbucks."

Really? She wanted to risk taking Nora into a Starbucks? Nora who ranted that any coffee place charging over 35 cents for a cup of coffee is a rip off, although she did acknowledge their excellent employee packages, but I couldn't remember ever actually entering a Starbucks with Nora. I had only snuck a few lattes with Kessia since I had gotten my license.

I pulled into the parking lot and Nora was the first to point out their enormous mermaid logo painted on the side of the building.

"What is this? A mermaid shrine? A mermaid church?" Nora inquired, adjusting her shell crown as we followed the amazing aroma inside.

"It's a coffee place," Amy explained. "Starbucks."

"Humans are certainly obsessed with mermaids," Nora noted.

We waited in line for a few minutes, grabbing snacks and juices for the car ride. When it was our turn at the register, I let Amy order first, and then I went for it, asking for a venti mocha latte. I'd be deliciously wired all day.

The Barista asked Nora what she would like next.

"I'd like to speak to the mermaid in charge."

"No mermaids here, but I'll get my manager." He disappeared behind a swinging door and Amy and I tried to lead Nora out of the store with zero luck. Nora wouldn't budge.

"I'm not leaving until I ensure no mermaids are being

bamboozled," she told us in my mom's voice. Her attorney voice.

The manager approached us with kind eyes and a massive smile, her hair pulled back in a ponytail, her suit all business. "How can I help you, Ladies?"

"Has that mermaid been compensated for her likeness?" Nora challenged, then grinned with her lips pierced together. I wondered if that was her court room face. It wasn't pleasant.

"Our logo? It's a drawing. I'm sure whoever drew her was paid handsomely. Starbucks abides by all industry standards." Thankfully the manager was mostly charming and only a tad patronizing.

"I'll be following up on this matter. Making sure there is no mermaid exploitation whatsoever happening here." It almost sounded like a threat. Nora definitely was in attorney mode, fired up.

"I can assure you, Ma'am. There is absolutely no mermaid exploitation at Starbucks. Thank you for caring about our logo."

Nora shook the manager's hand, "More people should."

Amy and I were able to leave with our snacks and delicious drinks, but Nora refused to indulge in a five-dollar cup of coffee. Were her pre-mermaid sensibilities returning? Had she seen her magic card bill? Would the list of frivolous charges blast the mermaid out of the water?

The car smelt divine as we made our way out of Denver.

"What was I like as a mom?" Nora asked, contemplative.

"Perfect," Amy grinned.

"Really? I want to know," she said. I stole glances at her in the rearview mirror, wondering if a part of her brain was re-connecting. Were Nora's synapses sparking?

"Strict…but fair. A good listener who offered good advice," I started, wanting to be honest even though it made me miss her to think about it. "Tired, but because you worked so hard, and helped so many people."

All the words I'd ever known all raced around and got stuck

in a traffic jam in my head. It was like the words I wanted to say were disobedient dogs, refusing to bark on command. I took deep breaths to sift through my thoughts. How was Nora as a mom? Altruistic. Nurturing. Difficult. Protective. How do you describe everything combined?

"Spread too thin," I sighed after I spurted it out, finally able to string a few words together.

"Amazing," Amy added, glaring at me in the mirror before smiling at Nora. "You were the best mom."

Nora laughed. "I was good and bad, huh?"

"She's right. You were an amazing mother. The best." I meant it.

Nora looked like she was tearing up, so I continued.

"Suffocating."

She smiled.

"Unrealistic expectations."

She laughed.

"Stingy," Amy shouted. And Nora roared.

"So, I was the worst mother in all of Columbus, Nebraska? You two are destined to be heroin addicts or con artists?"

"Yes." I grinned at her again. "You failed miserably."

"Lovely. You'll both have character."

"Am I part mermaid?" Amy asked.

"You both are." Nora said without hesitation. "You'd have to be, right?" She stared off again, seeking answers outside the window.

I felt I was. I felt that Nora loved Amy and I on a deep level, as our mother, even if she couldn't access that part of her brain. We were a part of her, her blood ran through our veins, and maybe we were a little bit mermaid. Maybe we all are.

Since the Starbuck's goodies kept us satiated, we didn't stop until Grand Junction about four hours from Denver. We gassed and ate, and each took potty breaks before making the choice to walk around Main Street until the circulation came back to our legs.

"I'll drive the next leg," Nora announced as she stretched, still looking at her legs like they were foreign to her.

"Thanks," I said, wanting to enjoy some time taking in the countryside as we travelled into Utah.

The scenery was magnificent with snowcapped mountains and trees. Dad called and I was able to talk to him for awhile since I wasn't driving. I also passed the phone to Amy so he was completely up to date on all of our welfare and adventures.

We drove to Richfield and then stopped for the night in Cedar City, Utah.

"We're making really good time," Amy said. "Too good."

She gave me a look that said, "Slow this trip down, I'm not ready to lose her." And I agreed. There was no need to NASCAR race to the finish line; we didn't have any deadlines.

"Let's have a good night. Gran was right. It's amazing here."

As we pulled into a hotel, Dr. Sy called mom. And she answered. Amy and I exchanged looks. We were going to have to confiscate mom's phone.

"Hello, Dr. Sy!" Nora chirped happily. "No, I'm going home now. You're welcome to visit. Do you snorkel or scuba dive? Hawaii's nice and the water's warm with plenty of turtles."

"Nora, are you suggesting we meet in Hawaii?" Amy and I could hear Dr. Sy's annoyance. "You need to return to Nebraska immediately. Let me talk to Emily."

"You can kayak...there's beautiful waterfalls," Nora's voice was weak, with a hint of sadness or dreariness. Her attorney confidence was gone again.

Amy took the phone from her gently and disconnected Dr. Sy.

"Does Hawaii have dolphins?" she asked, lacing her arm in Nora's and leading her into the hotel.

I tried to get all of our bags in one trip, but kept dropping one.

"Yes! Lots and lots of dolphin families," Nora perked up at the thought of her favorite sea creature.

"I'll meet you there," Amy replied, and I knew she meant it. I was pretty sure Amy would meet mom anywhere.

A bellman met us and relieved me of bag duty. "Checking in, Ladies?"

"Yes," Nora answered for us. "Emily, you'll come to Hawaii too, right?"

"Palm trees and coconuts. Count me in."

"I'm glad. I'm gonna miss you girls," Nora dipped into her sadness again. Amy and I exchanged worried glances.

After checking in at the front desk, the bellman led us and our bags to our room. He unloaded our bags, and opened the curtains, revealing the most breathtaking view.

"Hey, are you the mermaid family? I saw a clip on Yahoo."

"I don't think so," Nora responded, stepping out onto the balcony. Taking it all in. Amy and I followed.

"Yes," I said. "That's us. The Mermaid Phenomenon."

"I knew it!" he exclaimed. "Can I get a picture?

"Oh, okay." Nora pulled Amy and I close beside her. The bellman stepped in next to Nora.

"Cheese!" he said before ripping off about 12 shots.

"Can you take one of us, please?" Nora asked, handing him her phone.

We smiled for him, and then watched as he backed out of the room, already uploading his pic of us to his feed. For the first time, I wasn't embarrassed. What did I care if my mom was a mermaid and the world knew it?

"Oh, it's really good," Amy said, examining our first documented road trip pic. And she was right. The three of us were glowing as the sun set behind us. The view was amazing, and we were a family. Even if we only had a short amount of time left together.

I was terrified to go to sleep, worried that Amy and Nora would leave me stranded in the morning.

"I don't want to dump her off," I told Amy a thousand times.

"I believe you," she said, but I had seen her lie to Nora so much that I couldn't trust her entirely. Though we had the sister bond going, she had tried to leave me this morning and it was still fresh in my mind. Maybe even a delayed panic had set in, so I laid there listening to Nora's sound maker app for hours.

The ocean waves were like a lullaby, but even though I pretended I was in Hawaii, I couldn't reach oblivion. The truth was I was worried about Nora. Maybe Dr. Sy was right and I should bring her back to Nebraska. What if I was just making things worse?

I uploaded the pic of the three of us to my Instagram feed, not caring if anyone roasted me. Not caring what anyone else thought, or how many likes I got. It was my declaration of love for my sister and my mom and nothing else mattered. All I had was two more days with Nora and I didn't want to waste a second. #MermaidsForever

CHAPTER FIFTY-EIGHT

"You're in Las Vegas?!" Kessia screamed. "Without me?!?!"

"Yeah, I always thought my first time in Sin City would be with you," I watched her practically hyperventilate as we Skyped.

"I can't believe you didn't bring me with you. This is so something I would do!" She pouted and I could see she had painted her room a dark grey, almost black.

"I know, sorry."

Amy moved into view, interrupting our Skype session. "We'll be in Hollywood tomorrow." Did she realize that was like throwing water on a witch? Kessia would melt away with that news. Going to Hollywood was her dream.

"Noooooooo way...I'm dying," Kessia slithered from her seat to the ground and out of view. "Dying."

"Text me later," I yelled before closing the computer shut to join Amy and Nora, who had their heads pressed against our hotel room window. Looking down, I saw a miniature city of palm trees and splashes of pools. Paradise.

"That lazy river has my name on it," I said in a daze. "Who's with me?"

It took us almost twenty minutes to navigate around the MGM, not being used to the Las Vegas hotel mazes. It seemed like we had gone in circles, but once we stepped outside into the stifling hot air, we quickly found our pool home for the day, complete with pool side service.

While Amy and I enjoyed faux pina coladas, Nora was getting antsy.

"The desert is just so hot," she fanned herself. "I really need to get home."

"We had to let the tires cool," Amy said.

"Oh?"

"Yeah, they expand when it's hot. So we have to drive when it's dark," I jumped onto Amy's excuse and expanded.

"Oh, okay. I want us to be safe." Nora conceded.

When Nora got in the water to cool off, Amy and I huddled.

"We have a reservation at the Roosevelt in Hollywood. A pool suite. There's tons to do there, it will buy us at least 48 hours."

"Good job," I fist pumped her. "Dad knows?"

"Yeah. He's up to date...I just want to keep her a little bit longer. Okay?"

"I understand. I'm not ready to let go either." We didn't know what would happen when Nora's fluorescent pink toes touched the ocean, and though I knew it was inevitable, I wasn't in a rush to find out.

I finally understood Nora's attraction to the water.

Just a few days of hotel pools and I was hooked. I craved the release from gravity and the movement. It was as if it washed away my frustrations and insecurities. Like a snake shedding its skin, I became a new person underwater. I was free.

We walked up and down the Las Vegas strip for hours, shopping in the M&M store and staying cool inside the casinos. Nora was mesmerized by the water show in front of the Bellagio, so we sat there and ate ice cream and studied the eclectic groups of people shuffling past.

"Is it time to go?" Nora asked periodically.

"Nope, tires are still cooling," Amy said.

We ate dinner at the Top of the World, with another mind-blowing sunset. The desert sky was endless, bursting with color — a grand finale before welcoming the night lights. How had I never paid attention to the elements before? Was that just a part of growing up? Or was it Nora's influence?

"Oh, a full moon," Nora noted as we loaded into the car.

Had it been a month already since Nora's rain dance in Fred's yard? And six or seven weeks since my mom's accident? Nora had been a mermaid for so long; I was forgetting what she was like before the transition. I wondered if eventually Amy wouldn't remember our real mom at all. My chest heaved at the thought, and I held back tears, not wanting to grieve losing my mom until I had too.

AS WE DROVE across the desert, it was just us and the vast darkness in every direction, but up. The sky was lit by the enormous full moon and a trillion stars.

When we stopped at a rest stop, I lay on a park bench and took it in. The constellations, the twinkling. An infinity of wishes. Picking the brightest star I could find, and then closing my eyes, I made a wish.

My phone beeped, notifying me of a text.

I miss you. It was from José.

I shot up, looking for Nora and Amy.

Can we start over?

O.M.G. I wished Kessia was with me to tell me how to respond, but I knew she'd tell me to go for it. I wished I had a mom, like my real mom, in that moment. She'd know what to do. If he deserved another chance. If I should tell him off. If I should make him beg and plead for my forgiveness.

The perplexing thing was I hadn't wasted my wish on my

love life. I mean, yes, I saw there were a trillion stars and surely one could be used on José, but really, if I only got one wish, it had to be bigger than that. Bigger than us. No, I couldn't waste a wish on a boy, no matter how handsome, or how gushy he made my insides feel, even if his smile reminded me of the big dipper shining above me. If José and I were meant to be, we would have to work it out together. Not depend on astrological phenomenon.

Amy and Nora exited the restroom and sat on the bench besides me.

"José texted me," I burst out, so much for being cool.

"What did he say?" Nora asked.

I crossed my fingers her attorney side would show up, and then my mom. Who really wants love advice from a mermaid?

I showed her his texts.

"What does your heart say?" she asked.

"I don't know. I have such strong feelings for him, but I can't be his secret."

"Be honest with yourself...and him," she advised and I knew it was Nora at her core who was talking. Nora had always believed honesty was the most important virtue because we all lie to ourselves to make us feel better, but in the end it only hurts us. Lies just prolong and deepen our pain.

She was right. Whether it was Nora speaking or my mom from deep inside, I had to be honest. I had to be honest and let the pieces fall where they would. And so I told him how I felt about him and what I needed to move forward in a text.

Being vulnerable and exposed gave me the incontrollable need to make a bad joke, or anything to distract me from the feelings pulsing through my veins like liquid electricity.

"Your feelings can be your sails," Nora said, placing her hands on my shoulders, comforting me. "You'll learn when to make decisions with your heart, and when your mind needs to step in and overrule."

Five excruciating minutes went by before I heard back.

Check my Instagram, he sent.

"Hurry up!" Amy squealed as I switched apps. I searched his username and clicked on his account, holding my breath.

There was a picture of José hugging me for the world to see, or at least everyone who followed his private account. My eyes were closed and I was smiling the widest grin I've ever seen. We both had glitter all over us.

"He took a selfie of our mermaid blessing!" I remembered that moment. It was right after Nora tossed glitter on us, and I was savoring our bodies blending together. He captured it.

"He put hashtags," Amy said, "I'm impressed."

#MermaidBlessing #Happy4Ever #I(heart)Emily

The three of us jumped up and down together in the crisp night air as cars and trucks pulled in-and-out of the rest stop. A mother, her daughters, and the prospect of love instigated all by mermaid lore and a little luck. And we celebrated as we got back into the car and continued our trek to the Pacific Ocean, via a pit stop in the land of dreamers.

CHAPTER FIFTY-NINE

The Roosevelt was swanky, oozing the coolness of hipsters and people with money burning holes in their pockets. It was a combination of old school Hollywood history and updated coolness. Nora, Amy, and I were extremely out of place, but if the staff recognized us from the internet, no one seemed to care.

Nora's jewelry clanged as we walked silently behind the bellman, who looked like a movie star or a model. He opened the door to our suite and turned on the lights, placing our bags in the living room area and then leaving with his tip.

"I think someone's in here...snoring," I put my ear to the bedroom door cautiously. "Someone is definitely in there...We should go down to the front desk!"

"It's Dad," Amy said. Twirling her hair, acting deceptively innocent.

"Bart the Pirate is here?" Nora lit up, beyond excited.

"Yes!" Amy clapped, beyond happy with herself. Hey, I was impressed with her as well. Amy had pulled it off without either Nora or I knowing dad was meeting us.

Nora disappeared into the bedroom suite to join Bart. Amy

and I explored the room and went out to the pool, right outside our French doors.

"Dr. Sy's not going to jump out of the bushes, is she?" I feared the worst.

"No. Just Dad. He wanted to be here for the sendoff," she explained.

"Yeah, I get it."

Though she hadn't told me he was coming, I was relieved. I knew we were in over our heads if Nora lost it on the beach. It would be better if Dad was there.

"Any other surprises?" I dug, curious on what else Amy could pull out of a hat.

"One, but you'll like it," she grinned, pinching her lips together like Nora. She was her mini-me. My heart flinched as if snapped by a rubber band.

Amy and I swam in the moonlight, listening to the traffic and hubbub below, until the supermodel bellman came back and kicked us out of the pool, shaming us for not reading the "no swimming at night" rules.

We made the pull out couch into our bed for the rest of the night, sleeping as sisters with our parents in the other room. If felt so normal, like we were a family on vacation, but in reality, we were anything but. We were here to return our mother to the ocean and find out if she had the magnificent tail she yearned for. No, we were not a normal family on vacation at all.

WE WERE up with the sun, thanks to our wispy curtains, and Nora was up and ready to paint the town, in full mermaid garb per her usual. Since Bart was there, she wasn't as persistent to get home, wanting to enjoy another adventure before leaving her one, true love.

"The walk of fame should be fun, and Mann's Chinese Theater," she clapped her hands. "I hope we see movie stars!"

"Or a Kardashian or Jenner!" Kessia exclaimed, blasting through the door. She hugged me until we both fell over onto the couch. "You didn't think I'd miss this, right?!?!?!"

"Surprise," Amy said. And I hugged her like a boa constrictor squeezing its next meal.

Having my best friend with us made everything complete.

We traipsed around Hollywood like the tourists we were. We purchased t-shirts and souvenirs, explored the Kodak Theater mall, and took in the ambiance from the crowds. Nora called out the names on the Walk of Fame and asked Bart who each person was. He named off movies we'd never heard of and actors that were alive when they only had black and white TV. We stopped in front of the Mann's Chinese Theater and took a family plus Kessia photo.

A young couple asked to take their photo with Nora the Mermaid. And then a line formed. I didn't think it was due to her viral video, but more so her mermaid attire, particularly her shell and gemstone crown that sparkled in the California sun. Nora blended in with the SpongeBob and Batman who were also getting photos taken. People waited as if getting their picture with Santa at a mall, and they tipped her with dollar bills.

"Can I get one with your mermaid daughter too?" A girl asked, pointing to Kessia. With her extensions, I guess they did match, but jealously momentarily blinded me. Kessia ran to Nora's side, posing and hamming it up for the pictures.

Dad finally intervened, pulling Nora out of the crowd and back down Sunset Boulevard. We walked for a bit, and then I saw Nora give her tips to a homeless teenager sitting against a graffiti covered building, smoking an e-cigarette. She was even generous and selfless as a mermaid, her desire to help people ran deep.

With a collective group of sore feet, we retreated to the sanctuary of our hotel pool, which was alive and active. Bart went in to take a nap.

"Do you see anyone famous?" Kessia asked.

"I'm not sure. Everyone kind of looks like they're on TV." We were surrounded by absurdly beautiful people.

"I'm going to do a lap." Kessia took off to find someone who had graced a magazine cover, or at least an online homepage.

Amy and I both fell asleep on our lounge chairs, I was so tired that I didn't awake for two hours, complete with a pool of drool having formed on my towel. Thankfully, we were still in the shade. Kessia was nudging me with her foot.

"Wake up. Wake up." She echoed.

"I'm up." I tried to pull myself off the lounge chair.

"Hurry, come over here. Your mom is talking to someone," she warned.

I followed her over to the pool bar and stood next to Nora. A man with perfect hair, a glowing tan, and glowing white teeth was talking to her.

"Hi, I'm Emily, her daughter," I introduced myself to the stranger, who sent the heebie jeebies up my spine.

Mr. Perfect shook my hand, "Awe, the mermaid's daughter. I remember you from the video." It creeped me out to think of anyone like him watching me on the internet.

"Yeah..." I choked out.

"Why did you swim in your clothes?" He asked, pulling a miniature tablet from his shorts pocket and removing the tiny pen attached to the spiral bind.

"Are you a reporter?" Kessia interrupted.

"I am. For a star mag." He boasted like it was a good thing he was talking to my mother, but my protective radar alert was going off. He was up to no good.

"My mom's not a story," I said sounding like a defiant child.

"Emily, we were just talking. He wanted to know all about life in the Pacific." Nora defended him. Her instincts were apparently turned off entirely. Old Nora would have squished him like a cockroach.

"Yeah, well, interview over." I glared at him.

Mr. Perfect rose from his seat and protested, "I'm just doing my job. Mermaids are a hot topic. Especially this mermaid. I always get my story."

He winked at me. I was tempted to rip his eyelashes out.

"Did you swallow 432 Crest Whitening strips? Seriously, I'm blinded." Kessia blasted him. "What are you trying to do, lighten your intestines? You know, there are easier ways to bleach your colon."

We led Nora back to our hotel room as Mr. Perfect watched us the entire time. I had a feeling he would follow us. There was no way we could risk him following us to the ocean. We didn't know what was going to happen when Mom's feet touched the salt water, and the last thing we needed was for Nora's final breakdown to be front page news.

Amy, Kessia, and I held an emergency meeting in the suite's living room.

"We can leave in the middle of the night," Kessia suggested.

"He'll be there. He probably has an alarm on our door. And a deal with the valet to notify him if we leave."

"Yeah, he's at the pool and probably not a guest. He knows people," I assumed. The reporters on TV always had the hook up.

"We have to make mom unrecognizable," Amy said.

"An Un-Makeover!" Kessia announced, and we all agreed.

We filled Nora and Bart in on our plan and got to work de-mermaid-ing Nora, and sent Bart out for the necessary supplies. In true slumber party fashion, we all wore matching leggings and binged on junk food, delivered by yet another crazily good-looking hotel staffer. We debated if the employees here used head shots and sizzle reels to land their jobs.

Kessia snipped Nora's extensions free, unraveling them from the root, and gently removing the rainbow pieces. "I'm so keeping these."

Amy removed her nail polish from her toes, and I cut off her acrylic claws after soaking her hands in nail polish remover. I rubbed dish soap on her hands to get off the remaining glue, and then Amy painted her natural nails light beige.

"You okay, Nora?" I asked, worried that this sudden change was too much for her.

"I'm going home." She sighed and patted my hand. "I'm ready."

Kessia erased the henna tattoos, her blue eye shadow, and the glitter cream from her face and cleavage. I helped her remove her sea horse bauble necklace, and her collection of sea shell bracelets until Nora started to look like a normal person again. Bart returned with a pale yellow sundress and some sandals.

"You look beautiful," we all reassured her as she looked at herself in the mirror.

"A stranger," she said. "I don't look like me."

But she did look like her. She looked like our real mother.

"Okay, do me now!" Kessia barked. "I've always wanted to be a decoy." She held out her hands, waiting for the shell bracelets to be slipped on her. "And the crown. I want the biggest one she's got!"

CHAPTER SIXTY

K essia, as Nora the Mermaid, went out to the pool and made a spectacle of herself. She then traipsed through our hotel room, and out to the lobby of the hotel, giving the supermodel staff orders.

"I need an Uber. Or a taxi. I want to go to Rodeo Drive."

"Valet can help you," a staff member pointed, completely unfazed by Kessia's antics.

"I'm going to the most expensive shopping center in the world and buy the most expensive mermaid jewelry I can buy."

The staff member pointed again, returning to their magazine while Kessia clomped outside, whipping out her phone.

"He's following me," she said. "I can see his teeth from a mile away."

"Are you safe?" I asked. We were waiting in the hotel room, each of us staring at the cell phone listening to Kessia.

"Yeah, I'm in a yellow taxi headed towards Rodeo Drive. I've never been better!"

Amy and Nora hurried out of our room together, taking the elevator down to the lobby. Bart took the stairs and I went to the staff elevator by the pool so we could make sure no one else was following us. With all coasts clear, we met back at my car, which looked especially outdated and sad next to the fleet of Bentleys and Mercedes.

"Look at that Tesla," Dad gawked. "A beauty."

While everyone else was looking at the beautiful people and searching for celebrities, my dad was admiring the cars. I liked that about him.

He drove us towards the beach, taking the 101 freeway, and then switching onto the 10 West. As we got closer, I could feel the air getting damp, the breeze cooler. I shivered, looking at Amy and Nora cuddling in the back seat.

"We're almost there. I can feel it," Nora stated.

Dad continued along the 10 freeway until we entered a small tunnel. When we exited, we were on Pacific Coast Highway, the ocean just minutes away. We parked by the Santa Monica Pier where the beach was crowded, packed with families, tourists and locals. People rode bikes and roller skated on the pathway. The Pacific Park roller coaster spun up, back, and around the pier, full of thrill seekers enjoying this gorgeous sunshiny day.

"Take care of Fred for me. And the chicks. And Barney the goat," Nora started, kicking her sandals off and pressing her toes into the sand.

This was really happening. A numbness took over my body and mind, like static when the cable goes out.

Amy started to cry, and clung to Nora. I just stood there, watching a little boy fly a bright blue kite with his father. They were having a spectacular day at the beach while we were about to lose our mother.

"Don't be sad, Sweetheart. I will see you soon," Nora comforted Amy, holding back tears herself.

"Don't go," I choked, forcing my limbs forward and moving to hug her.

It was harder to say goodbye now that she looked like the Nora of my childhood.

"Just wait," she said. "When I touch the water, you'll finally see my tail."

She kissed my forehead.

"We're here for you, Nora." Dad said. "No matter what."

She embraced him, and then smiled.

"You're my soulmate, Bart the Pirate."

She skipped off ahead of us, eager to reach the shore. In only 20 yards, my mother's toes were going to touch the ice cold Pacific Ocean for the very first time.

"Dad, make her stop," Amy begged.

"I can't," he said, barely audible and stuffed his hands into his pant pockets.

We followed her as she raced to the water, pausing only briefly before she reached the shore to watch a family build a sandcastle. The entire setting was magical, a relatively perfect moment in time. She picked up a piece of sea weed and rubbed it in her hands. The wind whipped her hair around her face and she looked more beautiful than I had ever seen.

She turned to us one last time and waved.

"I love you!"

And then ran into the water, knee deep, the waves crashing around her. The California sun beating down, the sea gulls stealing potato chips and food off people's towels. Her sundress clung to her legs, the saltwater creeping up to her waist.

We waited. Too terrified to move. To speak. To breathe.

There was no tail.

Nora stood there with waves splashing her, staring out to sea.

I held my nervous sister who kept whispering, as if convincing herself, "Mommy's not a mermaid."

Nora kicked her legs around. Running deeper into the ocean. Her thighs were wet and she kicked some more until she was up to her waist.

"Dad!" I said, "Do something."

Nora dove into the water, splashing around. Kicking. Flailing.

I held Amy as Dad ran towards the shore. A lifeguard bolted towards the water and reached mom in a matter of seconds, his red shorts and tube a blur. He shouted at Dad to get out of his way.

"My tail!" I heard my mother scream. "My tail!"

The lifeguard guided mom out of the water. She was walking, but he was definitely holding her up. They walked up to the sand, navigating between children playing and sandcastles. Everyone was staring as the lifeguard helped Nora onto the sand, sitting her down and checking her vitals. He left her to return back to his post once he tapped Dad on the shoulder and was confident that she was okay.

And then Nora wailed.

The noise she made can only be compared to a wounded animal, taken down by a pack of lions, being torn apart as their next meal. Her entire body shook as she sobbed, not only for herself, but for the world as she knew it. Her pain reverberated through my soul as she fell lifeless onto the sand.

My mother wasn't a mermaid. She was heartbroken.

My dad went to her, and cradled her in his arms. She nuzzled into Dad's chest, heaving and sobbing some more.

We didn't know if she was still Nora the Mermaid, or if my mom had returned. Or if she was just completely gone.

CHAPTER SIXTY-ONE

A half hour later, Amy and I joined Dad and Nora on the sand. I wrapped my arms around her, unsure of what to expect.

"Emily," she said, and held me tight.

Crocodile tears dripped down my face. And I knew she was back. My mother had returned and I was so eternally grateful.

After a short while of re-connecting, Amy and I led the way towards the pier, taking Nora into the famous seafood chain, Bubba Gump's. No one dared to tell her she had been a vegan for the past six weeks. Nora was still shaking, and I wasn't sure it was from the freezing cold ocean water.

"Do you remember anything?" Amy asked, her curiosity on fire.

"I remember some stuff...vaguely. Maybe like a walking coma, I guess would be the only way I could describe it. I recall you painting my toenails," she smiled at her, and then to me, "...and you busting my chops."

"You thought you controlled the weather," I defended myself.

"It's like I was trying to micromanage the world. Keep

everyone from being hurt…and protecting myself from the unbearable pain I witness," Nora attempted to explain her thought process.

"That case broke your heart," Dad said. "And I did. I'm sorry, Nora. I promise to do better." He held mom's hand like he would never let go.

Nora sniffled. "All my cases break my heart." She squeezed Dad's hand, trying to find the right words. "Thank you. I will do better too."

"Dad ran around in a pirate costume. You two about killed me." I grinned, wanting to return to our old normal. Our family.

"I remember," she smirked. "…and I liked it." They kissed briefly, but enough to show their affection.

"There are going to be a lot of changes," she continued. "Necessary contract addenda."

"I figured all family contracts were pretty much null and void at this point." Would I have to confess that I had broken all her rules? All except the texting and driving contract.

"Not a chance, Emily. But we can make new contracts." She bounced between her attorney voice and mom tone. It was a tiny, but distinct difference, yet Amy and I knew them both well.

"Let's start with I can go to coffee without having to feel badly about starving children. I mean, I do feel badly, and I want to help, but I still want to go to out with my friends." I threw out, testing these new waters.

"Deal," Mom said and I wondered if it were some type of attorney trap to give in easily to the first demands. I'd have to be on my A game if mom's mind was back to peak performance.

"I want you to be more fun. Like when you were a mermaid…and do things with me," Amy confided.

"Promise." She hugged Amy tightly, "I want that too. More time together and definitely more fun."

"So, why a mermaid?" Dad asked. "You never were into cosplay or mermaid folklore before."

"Yeah, you didn't even have it right. Mermaids eat fish," Amy told her and Nora's hands covered her face in embarrassment. She slid them down slowly.

"I'm not sure, honestly. I guess I'll be doing a lot of work with Dr. Sy about it. A series of events perhaps. The escape of it. The complete departure from the ordinary. The freedom. All of it, possibly," she shrugged. "I may never know the why."

We all studied her, waiting for the mermaid to return. The mermaid that we had gotten used to and even sort of liked having around.

But the only mermaid that joined us was Kessia, still in my mom's sequin leggings and adorning the massive shell and gemstone crown. I had such a mixed reaction to seeing it again.

"I booked two parties…and I don't want to be a name dropper, but one is at Tori Spelling's youngest child's birthday!" Kessia applauded herself and her good fortune.

"That's crazy!" I said, loving that my best friend was fearless.

"Yeah, I'll make bank. This vacation is becoming so lucrative for me." She scooted into the booth next to me and told me all about her journey into Hollywood. Dad took care of the bill and Mom and Amy led us out the side door that led to the sand by the pier.

We walked on the beach as a family, enjoying the sunset over one of the most famous beaches. There weren't any celebrities or super models. Just normal people like us. We were a normal family again.

"I'm going to be okay," Nora reassured Amy again.

Dad and Mom held hands. Kessia and I motioned for Amy to stay back with us, giving them some space.

"I must have been so embarrassing," Nora shamed herself.

"You were hot!" Dad answered, pulling her in for a kiss.

Kessia captured the moment on her phone, posting it to her Instagram. "I hope someday I'm as disgustingly in love as your parents."

So did I. #RelationshipGoals #MermaidBlessings

EPILOGUE

M om made me present my case to her when we returned
home. We pretended the living room was a courthouse,
and I brought out my photo evidence first, explaining why Nora
the Mermaid was in fact my mother in the photos. I submitted
her diplomas and law degree next, along with letterhead and
business cards from Child Protective Services. She was
impressed with the genetic test results and that I had thought of
collecting DNA evidence.

Things became playful when mom cross examined me about
why she shouldn't stay a mermaid. "First, you'd have wrinkly
hands all the time living underwater."

"Yes, that sounds uncomfortable. But there are sexy pirates
at sea." She winked at my father.

"Please do not flirt with my expert witnesses," I scolded. "To
continue as to why you should not want to be a mermaid...bras.
Shell bras do not have amble support and can cause chaffing.
It's a huge problem."

Mom and Amy giggled on the couch together. "But really,
the biggest reason is because we missed you too much."

"Done! You've proven without a reasonable doubt that I am

not a mermaid. I am your mother." She jumped up and hugged me, "Great job, Em. You'll make an excellent attorney."

Mom and I continued to swim at the Y, although I didn't stick with the mermaid diet, and we didn't use the Y's mermaid tails. It was our mother-daughter thing to do together and we got to catch up before and after swimming since Nora was going back to work at CPS.

"I love it, Em. I truly love what I do," she said when I asked her to take more time off. "I'm gonna be home more and take less cases. But I'd die without my work."

"You said you'd die if I didn't take you to the Pacific Ocean," I reminded her.

"Yeah, and you did it. Thank you," she said before diving back underwater.

Tia blew a whistle, signaling that open swim was over. We changed in the locker room and then I waited for my mom by the front desk.

"How's it going?" I asked Tia. She looked stunning as always with her hair up in a maroon turban.

"Wonderful. I received two scholarships after all that media attention for my observations. Accolades are good." It was nice to see her happy, not that she wasn't before, but she was like sunshine now.

"That's amazing!" I soaked up her positive neurons.

"Yeah, and Polly's doing great."

"I'm glad." There weren't even words to describe how relieved I was that Polly was doing well. I couldn't stand the thought of Tia having more pain. Her and my mom had already been through so much. I wanted to help them. And I wanted to help others.

"We will hang out soon, I promise," she added as she exited. "I'll pick you up in my new wheels."

WANTING to make up for the time we had spent apart, José offered to help me clean the pig pens.

"This is pretty disgusting," he said, a shovel full of manure.

"Helps the veggies grow," I referenced the importance of pig poop in the environmental cycle.

"Yeah. I guess I'd be a horrible farmer," he kidded.

"But you'd look good in overalls," I flirted, still getting used to the fact that he was my real, public knowing, boyfriend. Savannah had even given us her blessing, in a friendship sisterly kind of way. And we had finally had that coffee, since my allergies were gone and all.

Fred, with newly green hair, and Gran, with her purple highlights, blasted away on an old motorcycle, but not before stopping to greet us.

"Go do something fun while you're young!" Gran shouted over the motor.

"Gran, you know how to drive a motorcycle?" I asked, concerned about their safety. Old people and motorcycle crashes probably wouldn't have a favorable outcome.

"Never too late to learn," she cackled and I let my fears go. If Gran and Fred were on an adventure, I had to stop worrying about what could go wrong and just accept what is.

Fred gave us a wave and the two rode off down the street.

It almost appeared as if everything in my life had gone back to normal; yet, it wasn't the same. Somehow, everything was different.

Six weeks of having my mother believe she was a mermaid changed me forever as a person, helping to make me into the woman I am becoming now. Gran ordered us all mermaid tail blankets in a variety of colors so we can enjoy mermaid family time on the couch while we watch movies or just hang out.

It was nice having my mother back, but she wasn't the same either. She was learning to relax and enjoy the moment more. To be present. Dad was busy too, but working less. Instead, he spent time planning adventures for the family as well as for he and my mom alone. It seems my parents were now looking forward to the golden years of their lives and continuing the rekindling of their romance.

Yes, life was normal again. For now, in this moment. Until the next twist of fate or catastrophe, because that is just how life works. For everyone.

And I hate to admit it, but it's the truth, sometimes I miss the mermaid.

A NOTE FROM THE AUTHOR

Thank you for reading THE MERMAID UPSTAIRS! If you'd like to write a review on the platform where you purchased this book, I'd be forever grateful.
For more information on THE MERMAID UPSTAIRS, including mermaid events, please visit TheMermaidUpstairs.com

COMING SOON:
SAME TIME YESTERDAY by Jami Lilo
For information on new releases, giveaways and freebies, please sign up for my newsletter here:
JamiLilo.com